THE DRAGONFLY

by

Rosemary Goodwin

WHISKEY CREEK PRESS

www.whiskeycreekpress.com

Published by
WHISKEY CREEK PRESS

Whiskey Creek Press
PO Box 51052
Casper, WY 82605-1052
www.whiskeycreekpress.com

ISBN 978-1-59374-102-0

Credits
Cover Artist: Jinger Heaston
Editor: E J Gilmer

Printed in the United States of America

Dedication

To my son, Gary, for his continued encouragement. Thanks!

PART I

The Dragonfly

Present Time
West Stow

In the pub's parking lot, cars nuzzled into the parking spaces next to the building, like suckling pigs on the teats of a sow.

Albert ("Just call me Al") White and his attractive wife, Catherine, known as Cathy to her friends, had edged their way out of the crowded pub. "See you Saturday," she called back over her shoulder to their friends.

"Race you to the car," Al dared as they darted out into the rainy night. He'd parked their car cautiously between two large vehicles.

"You're on." Cathy giggled as she pulled her jacket up over her head to protect her hair.

They opened the car doors and landed simultaneously with a flump onto the front seats. Cathy shook the rainwater from her coat. Some splashed onto Al.

"Sorry about that." She laughed.

"You really look it." Al grinned.

"Al, I'm shocked," Cathy said with mock offense.

He wiped the foggy windshield with his handkerchief. "Now, don't distract me from my driving."

"You're not driving yet! You haven't even turned the engine on," she snapped.

"Just warning you." He glanced at her. "Don't get nasty now."

"I apologize. Just tired."

"That's not an excuse."

He turned the key, and the engine purred to life. He popped a favorite CD into the player, and the car soon filled with the haunting, soulful melody of a clear-voiced pan flute.

"I'm going to go home the back way."

"Whatever." She pouted.

He exited the parking lot slowly, after checking in both directions for cars.

"I'll go through West Stow. Not so much traffic that way. It's hard to see in this rain." He squinted as the lights of an on-coming car glared in his eyes. "Must get new wipers this week."

"We'll light the fire as soon as we get home. This weather is disgusting. The cold goes right through to the bone," Cathy whined. She dug her hands inside her coat pockets and slumped down in her seat. "I wish we were back in the States where it's warm." She leaned her head back onto the seat's headrest, while the rhythm of the music entered and began to calm her whole being.

"We can't be on holiday all the time." Al eased the car around the sharp corners of the narrow country roads meant for use by horses and carts, and not for the horsepower of to-day's careening automobiles. Cathy slid upright in her seat.

She glanced through the gates as they drove by the old West Stow church, now almost deserted by the villagers, where generations of her family lay huddled in their eternal sleep in the churchyard. So many families moldered there at St. Mary's, beginning centuries ago, but with youngsters apparently no longer interested in the lovely old church, she wondered who would tend their graves when they were in there. Most of the churchyard had already become an overgrown tangle of weeds with ivy and gray lichen clinging to the gravestones, obliterating their owners' identities and eventually crumbling, returning to earthen minerals once more.

She thought of her mother, Janice. They should visit her tomorrow in town where she lived alone since the death of her husband. He'd been a farmer with a large farm, but it was sold off to pay debts.

Janice could be described as a timid woman brought up during World War II by an even more timid woman. She'd been raised to behave as all "good" girls should, in the opinion of the times.

As a young woman, Janice had vowed she would *not* raise her only child, a daughter, in a similar fashion. Consequently, Cathy grew into a happy, bubbly child, allowed to run in the rain without her shoes and climb trees with the boys. The child had a tremendous curiosity about the world and would ask grownups a hundred questions. Janice liked to think her little girl had grown into a self-assured, strong, and educated woman.

"Must drop by tomorrow to see Mum," she said.

Al mumbled in the affirmative, while concentrating on the road ahead. His parents had died recently and, since then, he'd become closer to his mother-in-law. Of course he worried about his mother-in-law living alone, but she had a stubborn streak, or was fiercely independent as Cathy insisted, and preferred to live by herself.

Al turned the car left at the row of thatched cottages, drove past the historic Tudor Village Hall and then by the stone cottage where her grandparents had lived. She remembered warm sunny days spent with her cousins in the gardens, playing shop or house in the huge clumps of lilac bushes.

"Seems like another time." She sighed.

"Whatever do you mean?"

"When I was a child," she chatted on, "out of sight of our parents, my cousins and I would lean over the sides of the old well and let down the pail on its chain into the dark water of the old-fashioned rock well."

Al gave a distracted, "Uh-huh."

"Then we'd turn the handle to raise the pail up again. We'd peer into the cool water, which sometimes contained a hitchhiker frog."

"Sounds like loads of fun."

"Then we'd half-fill sticky jam jars with water, put a hole in the lid with a nail, then we'd hang them with string high in the Victoria plum and greengage trees to entice robber wasps to certain demise."

"I love plums, too."

"That's not what I'm talking about!" She smacked him on the arm. "I'm recalling cherished childhood memories."

"Easy on the arm. It's raining cats and dogs, and I'm trying to concentrate on the road. Now be quiet for a while."

She sighed. Just thinking about those old days made her sad. The people now were merely ghosts, existing only in memories, just wisps of ectoplasm floating through time.

The car climbed the incline by the Crooked Chimney Row houses, which now had correct straight chimneys, and cruised along the road bordered with the forest of tall pines. The headlights hit a sign on the left hand side of the road. *Recreated Anglo-Saxon Village* it read, with a discreet arrow pointing into the darkness.

The rain had slowed down to a drizzle, and Al turned the wipers down to intermittent. Tall trees loomed over and marched along the sides of the road, making it seem like a leafy tunnel which dripped rain onto the tarmac below.

"I'd better look out for deer along here," he said quietly, almost to himself.

Cathy stared ahead into the darkness. Two orbs flashed back at them from the left side of the road. She gasped. "Watch out. Animal ahead! Did you see its eyes?"

"It's low to the ground—not a deer." He applied the brakes.

Suddenly, the orbs turned away from the headlights and the dark shape of a fox darted out into the road ahead of them.

"Damn it," Al yelled as he pulled the steering wheel to the right to avoid the animal. The tires squealed as they slid on the wet road surface. The car hurled sideways, thrown into a skid. He jerked the steering wheel to the left to come out of the skid, but he'd over-steered, and the car headed for the side of the road toward a ditch. He wrenched the steering wheel to the right again, but momentum took over and the car began to spin.

"Jam on your brakes," Cathy screamed. "Watch out for the bank!"

"I am," he shouted. "Just hold tight!"

He wrapped his hands around the steering wheel. They were in a death grip as he tried to point the wheels into the spin. The tires screeched. The force of the spin dragged the car across the road—balanced only on the two tires on the driver's side—the other two tires hung crazily in the air. The car seemed to be held there by an invisible thread. Then, with a crunching scrape, the airborne tires touched back to the ground. The car lurched across the road and straddled the roadside ditch with a loud thud.

She squeezed her eyelids closed to shut out the expected image of tangled car parts and smashed glass.

The car shuddered to a sudden stop with the crunch of metal scraping on metal as it folded onto itself. Glass fragments showered over them. Her body pitched toward the windshield, only to be punched in the chest by the inflating airbag. Searing pain ripped through her chest as her body twisted. Her skull bashed against the passenger-side window. The engine hissed steam. She smelled smoke. The headlights pierced the darkness.

"Al!" she screeched. Her lips swelled as she licked the warm liquid running into her mouth. Blood gushed out of a gash on her forehead. She looked over at her husband. His body slumped back in his seat, while his mouth gaped open and a dark line of blood ran down his chin. His legs were splayed at crazy angles to his body.

Cathy struggled to reach over to him, but was blocked by the steering wheel and dashboard that pinned him in his seat.

"Oh, my darling," she moaned. "Please don't leave me." She couldn't bring herself to say, "Don't die." To even think it would be fatalistic—so negative—no, she couldn't think that way. Her strong, virile husband seemed so fragile lying there injured.

A headache pounded inside her skull, and the surroundings began to spin. She must get some help; she must get an ambulance. The dashboard bulged inward toward her but she could still move her arms. She opened the door, which swung open with a creak, and then fumbled around her until she found the button to her seatbelt and pushed.

The belt released her and dumped her on the ground outside of the car. The vehicle rested at an angle, but not quite on its side. The engine hissed in a twisted knot of metal against two piles of dark grey and white flint rocks. She recognized it as part of the Anglo-Saxon village entrance.

Must be a gate, she thought. *Must crawl—can't stand up—too dizzy*. She told herself to crawl toward the wall where she could lean and flag down a passing car to help. They needed an ambulance.

Am I dreaming? It seemed moments ago that they were at the pub where the yeasty smell of beer and the noise of the crowd gathered in the low-ceilinged bar assailed them. A friend, Colonel Hambro, a red-cheeked, retired military man, had turned, raised his mug of beer, and yelled over the din. "We hope you're home for a while now."

Cathy had stared at the man's jacket, which jingled as he moved. Several shiny medals hung from faded ribbons on the tweed jacket's lapel. "Just been at a 'do' at the British Legion Hall," he explained as he patted the medals. "World War II commemoration. Well, anyway, so glad you two are back. It's pretty dull around here when you're away."

And it *was* a pleasure to see friends after several weeks away, although neither of them was anxious to return to the tedium of academe. They'd been granted a sabbatical from the university. For eight full weeks, they'd shed their duties. He'd been freed from imparting sociological studies such as Malinowski and the canoe-building traditions of the Trobianders in New Guinea to pimply, apathetic students.

Cathy had finished a challenging refresher course in Old English—a class she needed in order to scour the archives for her dissertation due the following academic year. *Alternative and Natural Medicine: Effects on a Society through History from Anglo-Saxon to Today's Population*. An ambitious title for what, she hoped, would be a significant sociological research paper.

But look at me now. Am I crazy? I'm crawling around in a ditch. As she pushed herself along the ground, she felt her hands and knees warm as they were cut and bled from the broken window glass in her path. She gathered more strength as she pulled her body away from the crushed metal. Everything spun around and around, so she lay still, face down in the mud.

Were the last weeks on vacation a dream, or is right now a dream?

She and Al had driven up and down the East coast of the U.S., sightseeing and poking around fascinating historical locations. They'd felt liberated, even giddy, like children just let out of school for the summer holidays. The newly discovered places provided them with a fresh perspective since so many locations in the U.S., like Jamestown and New England, were connected through history to their own county of Suffolk, back in England.

I must have imagined it all.

The headlights of an approaching car lit up the horrific scene. Steam and smoke rose from the wreck as the car screeched to a stop, and two men jumped out. One man ran over to the driver's broken window and stuck his hand through it and held his fingers on Al's neck.

"This one's a goner," he yelled over to other man who held a small cell phone to his ear as he shrieked out the details of the accident to the authorities.

Cathy stirred from her dizziness and shook her head to

Sign-Up for Lehigh Book Discussion Emails:

*Name	*Email Address
Nick Ladany	NLADANY@mac.com
John Evans	JADE@epix.net
Tom Molnano	tjmolnano@yahoo.com
Russ Flanagan	russflan@rcn.com

clear out the muddled thoughts. She patted her pant's pocket to make sure she had her own cell phone. *Good—it's there.*

"No. He can't be dead!" she tried to scream, but no sound escaped from her mouth. The words rumbled in her throat. "Help me. Please, help me."

This must be one of my nightmares again. I yell, but no one hears me. They haven't seen me over here. I must try to get up—wave my arms—something to attract their attention. Need an ambulance or a doctor for Al. He's still alive. These two are not doctors—just country clodhoppers with no medical training.

She gathered up all of her strength, pulled herself across the glass-littered mud, and through the stone entrance. Her fingers clutched at rocks, ripping her fingernails. Exhausted, sobbing, bleeding, and losing consciousness, she collapsed into a pitiful heap. The sounds of a flute floated through the steam and smoke.

The Dragonfly

PART II

The Dragonfly

Chapter 1

Anglo-Saxon village
620 AD

Cathy's head banged up and down on the hard surface of the floor of the vehicle. *Where was she? Where was Al? Please don't let him die*, she pled to any deity out there listening.

The rhythm pounded through her head. Jiggidy-jog, jiggidy-jog. She soon recognized the movement from her younger days of riding lessons. A horse was pulling the cart over bumpy terrain. As they passed through an opening in the trees, the moonlight shone down on the scene. Cathy surreptitiously looked around her. She was in a rough cart with three high sides mostly filled with chopped wood. She looked to the front of the cart, where the rump of a small horse, a little larger than a pony, bounced up and down between the shafts. An old man held the reins attached to the horse's bridle as he walked beside the animal leading it along the deeply rutted lane. Several small bells jingled on the harness, as though to warn anyone on the narrow road of the approaching group of villagers.

She turned her head to the side. Her nostrils filled with

the smell of sacking, just like the ones filled with potatoes at the vegetable shop. The material scraped her skin as her face grazed it with each shift of her body.

Blood still caked her forehead, and the cuts on her hands and knees stung.

She raised herself onto an elbow and reached upward with her other hand to the top of the board on the side of the cart and poked her head above the rim.

Several men of various ages shuffled alongside the huge solid-wood wheels. They had long, bedraggled hair, and wore blanket-like cloaks. *Ponchos? Who were these people and where was she?* Bewildered, she dropped back down onto the bottom of the cart.

She'd been picked up from the roadside by a bunch of hippies! They must be camped out in the forest somewhere away from prying eyes. Now no one would ever find her. She lay back down on the floor of the cart and tried to control her breathing, which came in panicked gasps. She feared they would hold her for a ransom, or something worse.

The old man leading the horse rang a bell as he walked. Another played an odd melody on a pan flute. The music drifted through the misty air of the forest. The men called back and forth to each other, and she strained her ears to catch what they said.

"*Wifmann*," mumbled one man, "*wohful*."

The words were strange and guttural—almost Germanic. Although dumbfounded, Cathy understood what they were saying. Could she be wrong? Could this band of hippie misfits really be speaking Old English? She'd heard the ancient words for "woman wicked."

"*Na wifmann wohful,*" the old man yelled back. "She's not a wicked woman."

Her vocabulary words from the class she'd just taken were fresh in her mind. She wasn't mistaken. They *were* conversing in Old English.

The old man raised his fist as a signal to the others to come to a halt. He let go of the horse's reins, walked back and peered at the woman sprawled on the blanket. He held out his hand to help her as she struggled to sit up. He called out to the others, "*Séo forht cwen aweccan*—the frightened woman is awake."

She dangled her legs over the front of the cart and immediately felt dizzy. The old man said, "*Bealo*. Injury," as he touched the gash on her head. His hand lingered in her hair, stroking the curls.

"Don't touch me." Cathy pushed his hand away. "Who are you?"

She spun her head around to face the others. "Are you Anglo-Saxon re-enactors from the village?"

No reaction from the men. Either they were ignoring her, or didn't understand plain English.

"*Hael wastu?* How are you?" the old man said.

"I am injured," she answered in their language. *Hell, I might as well play their game too,* she told herself. *They aren't the only ones who know the old language.* "My husband and I were in an accident. Two men were calling for medical help, and that is the last thing I remember."

"Woman, I know not what you are saying." A frown crossed his forehead.

"Then you must have found me and put me into your cart. Did you see my husband? I must find him," she continued.

"We found you near the road on which we travel back to our village, Stow."

"Do you work at the village?" she asked.

"Everyone works in our village." He appeared confused at her question.

"Well, that is the answer. You are re-enactors. But why speak in Old English?"

"I do not understand. What is that you call Old English?"

She laughed, but held her arms across her chest to buffer the aching muscles.

"And I really do admire how you keep in character, even down to using the old language."

"You speak about such strange things, woman. Sit back in the cart," the old man commanded. "We must hurry along our journey. Our families will be worried about us if we are too late getting home."

Cathy inched backwards into the cart. He clicked with his mouth, and the horse resumed its pace along the rutted lane. She moved onto the scratchy blanket again and leaned on the logs for support. As soon as they arrived at the village, she'd call the police to pick her up and take her to the hospital. She was concerned for her own safety. Who knew what these men were up to? *Al must be at the emergency room by now.*

She pulled the small phone out of her pocket and flipped the top open. It broke into two pieces in her hands—it didn't light up, or sign on with the happy jingle she'd programmed it to do. Nothing. Silence. It was dead; she felt lost. No way to contact her husband. *This is a nightmare.*

The acrid smell of wood smoke filled the air. In the moonlight, the outlines of small buildings appeared as silhouettes clustered on a small hill. The cart rumbled along the path as Cathy peered over the sides. The whole village looked different. *Maybe I'm in a different part of the village.*

Strange-looking, long-haired pigs grunted from their enclosure. *Isn't this where the parking lot usually is?*

Cows lowed softly from the neighboring meadow. *The Welcome Center should be there instead. What's going on?*

A pack of dogs ran toward them, barking furiously.

The cart jolted to a stop, which caused her to roll out of the back of the cart onto the muddy earth. She screamed in pain as she hit the ground. Her body bore so many cuts and bruises, and this sudden dumping added even more.

One of the younger men held out his hand, and she grabbed hold as he hauled her to her feet. "*Manig hearm.* She has injuries," he said as he steadied her.

"Leave her. Slaves are not to be helped," the old man yelled.

"What do you mean, slave?" she snapped. She felt faint. "You are taking your acting parts too far. I will not be a slave."

"You have no choice. You appear to be from a far village. Your hair is dark and your eyes are almost black. Your kind is a remnant of the Romans, long gone, but whose issue remains. Our villages are those of pale skin, eyes and hair. Not dark like yours. You are now our slave and will obey all commands."

"No, I will not."

The young man grabbed the blanket from the cart and gently draped it around her shoulders like a shawl. Her neck and face instantly itched.

The old man pushed her ahead of him. Cathy tripped on the ruts in the road. Her bruised and cut legs screamed pain with every stumble.

"No need for cruelty, Pendor," the young man grunted as he followed them.

Pendor spun around to face the younger one. "The woman is a slave. She will do slaves' work and live in the slaves' house. It appears you think soft, like a maiden, Cuthbert," he mocked.

Cuthbert grimaced and spat on the ground. He led the horse away down the lane to the pasture before slapping the hindquarters of the animal. The freed animal bolted through the opening and pranced over to the huddle of horses on the opposite side of the meadow. Puffs of steam hung over their heads as they whinnied in greeting.

A figure moved toward them carrying a lamp. Pendor prodded Cathy forward with a stick. The flame in the lamp guttered as the fat burned and revealed the face of an old woman.

"What have you here?" the old hag asked in a raspy voice. She hacked out a bronchial cough and spat on the ground.

"Found you a new slave, Etheldreda," announced Pendor. "She'll work for you and no one else in the village."

The woman's grey hair hung in greasy rattails. She poked her face into Cathy's and hissed her breath through brown and worn-down teeth. "Call me Ethel," she said.

Good Lord! Halitosis. This filthy, old woman is too real to be a re-enactor. This must be a dream. Or am I dead? Cathy waved her hand in front of her nose and shrank back away from the breath that stank like dung. The old woman reached over and tugged on Cathy's hair. *"Softe and clæne. Welig wifmann.* She is soft and clean like a rich woman."

Pendor shrugged his shoulders and walked away.

Ethel grunted and hitched up the long garment she wore to free it from the mud. She held the lamp up to shine a feeble light on the way and grabbed Cathy's arm, painfully pinching it, as she pulled her along the pathway in the direction of a small building.

"Ow!" Cathy yelled. "Stop squeezing me."

The old woman stopped at a crude wooden door, put a finger through a hole and lifted the latch on the inside. She shoved her new possession into the hovel.

Cathy stumbled over the door's threshold. Her foot hit some stones in the center of the room, which made her lose her balance. She cried out in pain as her shoulder hit a wood pole in the dark, before landing on a pile of straw. "Where is the light?" she sobbed out in the old language.

Lit by the moonlight that pierced the darkness, Ethel placed the lamp on the plank floor next to a circle of stones. The stones surrounded a clay pit containing ashes of a previous fire.

"I will make new fire." Ethel grabbed a handful of straw from the corner of the room, touched it to the lamp's flame and carefully placed it under a pile of kindling which she laid criss-cross within the pit. Flames licked the dry slivers of wood, which soon crackled and snapped as the fire came alive. She tossed some logs onto the burning heap. Each flame's shadow danced on the bare wood walls of the hut.

Smoke from the fire swirled up into the heights of the roof, where it escaped through the thatch. Cathy's eyes began to water and sting from the smoke. She feared for her sensitive sinuses. *No wonder the woman had a hacking cough.*

Ethel came closer to her, crouched down and stared at her with eyes covered with pale-blue cataracts. "Where are you from?" she asked.

"I am not sure," Cathy said quietly, "but right now, I'm exhausted and still bleeding from my cuts. I have to lie down and rest."

The woman grunted and nodded as she threw a dirty covering over a pile of dried heather and straw on one side of the hut and then handed her a rough blanket. Cathy lowered herself gingerly onto the primitive bed and pulled the blanket up to her neck. Fear crept into her being as she realized this village wasn't the recreated village she knew. Thoughts swirled around inside her head.

Where am I? What happened to me? Am I dead? Is this a dream? Am I in a parallel universe? Am I in another dimension parallel to our universe? Cathy thought back to a lecture she and Al had attended on the new "string theory," where it is thought that time and dimensions bend and even operate simultaneously. *Did the accident cause me to morph into another parallel world, identical to our universe but operating in a different time period? Where is Al?*

She wished she hadn't been so impatient and snappy with Al. She was now stuck in this dream, or whatever it was. Unless she was dead, how would she return to her husband, her one love?

She could hardly wait for daylight; she hurt—a lot. In the light, she might be able to determine what she should do next. Also, she'd need water to wash her wounds and look at her face for the first time since the accident. Her head ached. So many questions circled inside her head. She'd sort things out tomorrow.

Exhausted and aching, she fell into a fitful sleep, jerking awake gripped with fear for her future, then falling back into a nightmare-filled slumber.

Chapter 2

Cathy woke up itching all over. Daylight was creeping into the sky, but the south-facing window and door didn't give her enough light to see what made her itch. She crawled out of the bed and stepped outside into the sunlight. Fleas hopped all over her legs and arms and, as she glanced back at the bed, she saw the blanket move. *Bed bugs?*

"Disgusting," she cried out as she slapped herself to brush off the fleas.

At that moment, Ethel came around the corner. The old woman's face wore the same dirt from the night before. Dried mud caked and flaked off her skirt.

"What is wrong?"

"My bed is full of fleas. I've been bitten all over," Cathy snapped shaking her skirt.

"From the dogs," Ethel answered. "Shake them out of your clothing."

"The heather and straw should be taken out and burned. It's full of bed bugs."

"It would not make a difference. Dogs with fleas sleep in all of the beds," Ethel answered with disinterest. "The other insects are always here."

Cathy decided it would be useless to argue the point. "I'm hungry. My stomach is growling, and my clothes smell of blood and mud. I would like to wash them, but I'll need a blanket or something to cover me up while my clothes dry."

The old woman nodded toward a barrel at the side of the building. Cathy dropped a wooden bucket into the barrel and struggled to pull it out by its rope handle, full of water. Her sore muscles screamed with the exertion. She poured the water into the large metal cauldron hanging over the fire. Ethel snapped some twigs and pushed them into the fire to encourage larger flames. When the flames snapped and hissed, Cathy added some larger pieces of wood and a small log onto the fire. The water soon bubbled hot.

Outside, Ethel yelled to two young boys, "Go down to the river and bring back water to fill up this barrel."

Cathy made a mental note that it was dirty river water, not rain water, in the barrel.

Cathy stripped off her slacks and top and dumped them in a heap on the floor. Ethel returned with a basin of cool water and a bar of animal-fat soap she placed on a three-legged stool. She had some strips of cloth draped over her left arm. She handed the strips to Cathy.

Cathy added some hot water to the cool water in the basin and rubbed soap onto one strip of cloth. She dabbed at the dried blood of the cuts on her face and arms. The touch of water stung and the cuts began to bleed again as the scabs were loosened. Flies flew around her, some landing on the dried blood on her wounds.

"Do not destroy these in the fire," Ethel warned her. "These strips must be washed for you to use again."

"What do you mean?"

"During each moon's bleeding, you will wear these strips

stuffed with moss."

"Of course." *I want to go back to the present and all of the comforts that go with the modern lifestyle. I can't endure this,* she screamed on the inside.

Ethel shooed at the flies buzzing around the bloody clothes. "I shall bring you new clothes," she muttered as she picked up Cathy's slacks and top and dipped them into the boiling water in the cauldron over the fire. Cathy shuddered when she saw her wool slacks and pullover swirling in the boiling water. *They'll fit a small child now.* After a couple of minutes, Ethel draped the steaming clothes over a sturdy stick and carried them outside.

Cathy watched Ethel as she spread the clothing over a shrub growing against the wall of the house. The old woman disappeared among the huddle of buildings, but soon returned with a hunk of bread smeared with bacon grease balanced on top of a mug of liquid that smelled like beer. Cathy murmured thanks as she took the bread and shoved it hungrily into her mouth. Ethel handed her the clothing draped over her other arm. "Wear these," she said.

Cathy swallowed the drink and handed the mug to Ethel. "Tell me about a woman's life in your village." She held up the fresh garments, then arranged them on a bench. She was curious to see whether history had recorded the correct reality of life in that period of time.

"What does it mean to you, slave?" the old woman answered.

"If I am to spend my life here in your village, I need to know how women are treated."

"You are a slave. You will work in the fields. You will not be treated as a villager here."

"I realize that. For now, but I'll soon show everyone I'm

not slave material."

Ethel hissed through her decayed teeth.

Cathy turned to the pile of clothing. She held up a long, tube-like tunic and slipped it over her head and shoulders. She slid her feet into the pair of soft suede sandals with round toes and laces which criss-crossed up the front of her legs.

Ethel reached into a pouch hanging from her belt and handed her a comb fashioned from bone.

"You will find a comb important to you when you are infested with lice. You may keep it as your own. We do not always have larkspur to make a rinse to kill lice in the hair. You must then use your comb," Ethel said with a sniff.

Cathy shuddered at the thought of living creatures crawling through her hair and clothing.

"You wanted to know about a woman's life here in the village?" Ethel continued. "Women marry a man of their choosing, unlike other villages far up north, where a woman has to marry the man chosen by her parents or family."

"Interesting." Cathy murmured.

Ethel ignored her and continued, "Many women die because of miscarriages and fever from childbirth. Woden, the king of the gods, sends evil elves to shoot us with arrows filled with pain. Life is brief between birth and death."

Cathy nodded her acknowledgement.

"In our time, a woman is seen as powerful, serves as head of the household, and makes sure the community survives."

"Fascinating," said Cathy. "It's a pity such things do not survive and takes centuries to become known as the *freedom,* the freedom, of women."

Ethel merely stared. Then, satisfied that her new charge was now refreshed and dressed in clean clothing once more, Ethel beckoned Cathy to follow her. "Come with me. We go to my family's house."

Cathy hiked up her long dress and tightened the belt to keep it in place. Ethel preceded her, hopscotching around puddles until they reached one of the thatched houses.

"This is my home," Ethel said as she turned to face Cathy. "You will sleep here so I can watch you. So you won't escape. My sister, her children, and I live together here in my living house. There are many more people in my family, but they live in other houses beside ours."

She went through the doorway and stalked to the opposite wall, where she pulled aside a curtain that covered the sleeping pallet of a young woman.

"Get up, Bega, you lazy wench. You are just like your *modor*—mother," yelled Ethel as she kicked the woman in the behind.

"Ow!" screamed Bega. She crawled off the straw-filled bed and grabbed her shawl hanging from a nail on the post.

Cathy's eyes began to water again as wood smoke rose off the fire into the small loft. The loft took up half of the roof area where meat in sacking bags hung in the smoky rafters.

"Get to the weaving house," Ethel snarled at Bega. "She is to finish some cloth needed for the wedding feast tables." She turned to Cathy. "The girl is the daughter of my sister. You go with her, and she will teach you how to *bregdan*—weave. You have to earn your keep."

Bega slunk by the old woman as she ran her hands through her ratty hair and picked out stray bits of hay. She mumbled to Cathy to follow her, and the two women trotted toward the group of buildings.

Bega pulled Cathy by her sleeve into one of the huts grouped in a circle.

"Why are the huts in a circle?" asked Cathy.

"Do not ask questions," snapped Bega.

"But I need to know these things."

"I suppose so. The buildings in this circle are living houses and the workshops belong to our family, of which Ethel is an elder. In the middle," Bega explained reluctantly, "is the building where the family eat their meals and discuss important matters."

Cathy peered around, noting other circles of buildings dotting the open ground of the village.

They entered the weaving house, where a large, upright loom stood against the wall in the light let in by the open door.

"Ethel said the fabric is for a wedding feast. When is it to be held?"

Bega glared at Cathy. "If you must know, it is after the next moon. So I have plenty of time to finish my weaving." Bega sat on a stool. "The wedding is to be of my sister, Annis, and a man named Gerhardt from the other side of the village. They had a handfasting about a year ago."

The girl pulled some long threads of flax linen from a basket on the floor and handed one to Cathy.

She pushed Cathy onto a stool next to hers. "Watch me." She tied one end of a thread around the top pole of the loom. Then she took a clay donut-shaped weight and threaded the string through the hole in the middle of the weight and let it drop. Cathy soon tied threads as quickly as Bega and, in about thirty minutes, the threads were all hanging, weighted, down near the floor.

"Now what?" Cathy asked.

"You now weave across with another thread in and out from one side to the other side. Simple," said Bega. "When you finish a row, you beat it down close to the previous row with the beater."

"Seems easy."

"It is *not* easy. And it gets tiresome."

She'd only woven one thread and her arm muscles were burning already. Bega smirked as Cathy rubbed her arms.

"See the small tablet loom hanging on the wall over there?" Bega pointed to a wooden contraption on a nail. "With that, we make pretty braids using dyed threads."

"Promise you'll include me when you make the next lots of dye."

"Oh, you will be included. It will be one of your jobs," Bega shot back.

"Oh, nice." Cathy didn't intend to stay in the village very long. If she could only figure out a way to get back to her old life with her husband, she'd be gone in a flash. Maybe she could sing a special chant, or use a magic spell. She'd ask Ethel if she knew of any magicians.

After living in this village and speaking in Old English for a whole day, she was now convinced she had traveled back in time. The whole premise was far-fetched, even unbelievable. How could she bounce back in time? She had to find her way back home before she went insane.

Why couldn't she have been thrown back into history during the Roman period in Britain, with forced hot-air grates in the floor, real plumbing, and heated bathing pools? Instead, she'd arrived a couple of hundreds of years later at an Anglo-Saxon village inhabited by dirty, rough-living pagans, and that's where fate had dumped her—*thank you very much*.

Chapter 3

Bega ignored her and became busy at her weaving. Since there was only one loom, Cathy soon tired of watching the girl. When Bega turned away to add more linen threads, Cathy slipped silently out of the hut.

It was now *middæg*—noon—and the sky looked like a painting of a picture-perfect blue, with fluffy clouds scudding across the heavens over the village below. A flock of speckled starlings scratched the soil in the field next to the lane in search of insects. Carrion crows cawed from the scrubby pine trees, while house sparrows chattered from the roofs as they, too, searched for insects, but in the thatching. Chickens scattered as she walked among them and separated the flock. A dog loped along the worn dirt path; a cat sat on a doorstep washing its paw.

She wandered through the small village where its inhabitants busied themselves with their daily chores. A milkmaid carried two pails of milk dangling on the ends of the chains attached to a wooden yoke she wore around her shoulders. A young man chopped and split logs; another wove a fish trap. The carpenter nodded a good morning as he turned bowls on a springy pole lathe, and a group of teenage girls poured animal fat into clay forms to fashion candles. Two children walked by, each carrying a willow basket filled with hens' eggs they'd collected from the chicken houses. An elderly woman held a basket between her knees as she wove the reeds in and out.

Cathy slowly approached a three-sided building with the open side housing a furnace. A young boy rested next to the bellows pointed into the furnace. A big pile of black charcoal sat next to the furnace ready to be piled into the red-hot mouth of fire. Blacksmith tools lined the back wall.

The man, tall and blonde, had his back to her. His discarded tunic hung on a peg on the wall, and he wore tight, brown trousers lashed to his legs with lengths of hide. He oozed maleness, and despite Cathy's injuries, a shiver went through her hips and down her legs. His naked torso formed a large triangle from his broad shoulders to his narrow hips.

His huge, hard, muscular arms, tanned golden brown, glistened with sweat as he struck the red-hot metal with a hammer. With each swing of the hammer, his shiny abdominal muscles rippled, like undulating waves on a wind-swept sand dune. The metal rang out with each blow. He inspected the shape, and, apparently satisfied with the completed item, turned and plunged it into a bucket of water.

He looked up through the steam rising as the hot iron cooled. A smile crept up on his lips. He stared unashamedly at Cathy, riveted to the spot.

"Al?" she said quietly. "Is it you?"

"No, young maiden, I am called Ædelbert." He stared at her slowly, beginning at her face, slowing even more at her breasts and then down to her feet, drinking in every inch of her. His gaze feasted upon her body. She enjoyed the feeling.

"Do you mind if I call you Ed for short?" She approached

him.

"I do not object to being named Ed." He held out his hand to her.

She touched his hand in friendship.

"What should I call you, maiden?"

"My name is Catherine, but you may call me Cathy." Her face heated up as she looked down at her feet. *What? I can't believe I'm bashful.*

She raised her head. He still stared at her.

"You have a handsome face. You are dark. Dark hair and eyes. Not like our village people. Are you a Roman woman?"

"No, I'm not," she barked, unthinking. The assumption was tiresome how everyone thought of her as a Romano-British peasant because of the color of her hair and eyes. "I apologize," she quickly added.

He frowned at her and stepped over to the furnace. With a nod of his head, he directed the young boy to blow air through the bellows onto the hot coals. Ed held the metal piece with long tongs in the heat.

"If you are not from here, then where are you from?"

"I'm from the future. I'm from this place, only more than a thousand years from now. I do not know how I got here so don't ask," she snapped.

"Really?" He smirked. "We have been told you are a mere slave and belong to Ethel." He looked over the metal in the tongs. "You are not dreaming, are you?"

"Absolutely not. I'm only a slave temporarily. I intend to show everyone I'm of a higher status than a slave. I have knowledge of many things to come." Cathy embarrassed herself—she sounded like an indignant child.

"It will be difficult to change the opinions of the village elders," he answered. He seemed disinterested as he dumped the hot metal into the cool water where it sizzled.

"I'll manage, thank you," Cathy answered. Then after a long pause, she said, "What are you making?"

He swung around quickly, as though surprised she was still there.

"A new blade for a plow. It is needed for the plowing of the bean field. I just completed an axe for my father." He pointed to an axe head on his work bench.

He turned to the boy. "Here, take this bucket down to the river and bring me more water." The boy ran off toward the river, whistling as he swung the wooden bucket in an arc.

The blacksmith bent to splash water on his face and chest. Cathy admired his body. *He looks like one of those sexy hunks depicted on the covers of romance novels.* Her friends would be so envious—if she ever got back to see them.

Several people scurried past them, each one carrying a bundle. They headed toward the community's main hall in the center of the village, chatting to each other as they hastened on their way.

"What's going on?" Cathy asked Ed.

"Must be Cedric, the Trader. He has not been here for a while." He took his shirt off the peg on the wall, but didn't put it on. Instead, he carried it in his left hand as he extended his right hand to Cathy as an invitation. "Slave woman," he said with a grin, "would you like to come along to the great hall and see what all the commotion is about?"

"Yes, I would like to." Cathy ignored the snide remark.

They reached the great hall, pushed through the crowd around the door and stepped into the building. A skinny man—Cedric, she assumed—carefully opened up his blanket and spread it out in the center of the floor. He told the crowd that he had just returned from *Gipeswic*, the next large town in Suffolk, about thirty miles east from Stow. Cathy recognized the town's name, Ipswich, from the pronunciation *Yip-es-witch*.

The trader had set out his wares on the blanket for everyone to see and, hopefully, trade for articles they had.

"I have gold brooches, colored glass beads, cowry shells, and containers of salt from the coast," Cedric called out as he broke open a container of salt to reveal a hard lump of salt from which he offered samples to taste.

He also had belt buckles, brooches, sleeve and wrist clasps made from bronze, with complicated Celtic-styled swirls and knots. The village's families lined up outside of the hall door, waiting for their chance to do business with Cedric. They carried skeins of dyed wool, tanned hides, combs made from bone and antlers, and pottery.

Ed picked up a string of amethysts and held it next to Cathy's face.

"These would look beautiful upon your skin," he said. His hand brushed her cheek. She stepped backward to avoid further contact. His touch brought forth too many emotions she didn't have the strength to handle right now. She found him dangerously attractive—she had to stay away from him. She longed for her husband's touch, but she could easily be tempted by this testosterone-loaded man.

Ed watched her through narrowed eyes as he kept his distance. He returned the necklace to the blanket and picked up a delicate cross on a gold chain. He held it up. "Look, this is the symbol of the new religion."

She moved closer to him to inspect what he had in his hand. "It's called a crucifix or a cross. It is how Jesus Christ was put to death. His enemies nailed him to a cross through his hands and feet." Not knowing anything about his intelligence, she didn't want to make her answer too complicated for him.

"You seem to have knowledge of this new god named Jesus." He examined the crucifix closer.

"The worship of Jesus is called Christianity."

He looked interested. "One evening, as we gather around the fire, would you tell my family about this new religion?"

"Yes, I'll be happy to tell you what I know." She continued to stroll around the blanket as she gazed at the jewelry and other items spread out for inspection.

His hand, rough and calloused, touched her arm, softly rubbing her skin. She didn't pull away this time and let it linger there until he moved to pull his shirt over his head.

She stood close to him, breathing him in. "Do you have a large family?"

"Everyone has a large family." He chuckled.

"Let me rephrase the question. Are you a married man?"

"No, I am not."

"Nor are you betrothed?" She needed to ensure she'd asked every question possible. If someone asked, she couldn't explain why she had an interest in this man's status. *I'm ashamed of myself. I have a husband already and here I am cozying up to this hunk.*

"No, I am not betrothed. I am free as a bird." He smiled at her. His face, a golden tan, contrasted with his pure white and perfect teeth.

Must be genetics because there's no dentist here, and the rest of the villagers have nasty teeth.

They left the shadow of the great hall and went outside into the bright sunshine. Ed's longer legs put him a few paces ahead of her, but he turned toward her as they walked.

"Speaking of being free as a bird," he said, "would you like to see my hunting bird?"

"Yes, sounds interesting." Cathy felt like she'd just been

asked to "see my etchings." Ethel would probably be angry that her slave had walked away from the weaving house and not returned, but she didn't care—she resented being treated as a possession.

"Then follow me. It is a distance from here. My young cousin is working with the bird in the woods next to the sheep meadow."

"Where is the meadow?"

He pointed to the north.

Cathy hitched up her *cyrtel* to avoid tripping on it in the dusty lane. A large hare ran across her path, making her jump. Cathy huffed and puffed as she attempted to catch up with Ed, but his long legs were outpacing her. He stopped and waited in the middle of the lane as she caught up with him. She panted to catch her breath.

"The clay pit is over there." He pointed to a dip in the land as he slowed his pace in order for her to recover from the brisk walk.

"Hail, Wybert," Ed called out to the man painting pots at the clay pit.

The busy potter waved in recognition as the couple approached, then dipped a paint brush into a horn containing black liquid and began to paint in the grooves of a newly fired pot.

"What are you using?" she asked, curious.

"*Blæc*—black ink," he replied.

This intrigued her. She'd been wondering how she could keep a journal of her stay at the village. She could use a deer hide as paper, but she needed ink. Now she would discover the recipe.

"How is it made?"

"From egg whites mixed with soot and then stirred with

honey to make it into a smooth paste," he answered, looking up from his decorating.

"Let us go on," Ed called out. He'd already strode away from the clay pit. He looked bored. Cathy hurried after him.

"Thanks," she called to Wybert over her shoulder.

They soon arrived at the meadow.

"You will not be afraid of my hunting bird, will you? It is a *fealcen*." He stared into her eyes, direct and unabashed, which made her blush. *Why am I blushing like a teenager again?* It had been a while since she'd had a man pay attention to her. How long would she stay here in the village? Would she remain there permanently? Should she find a new husband—or at least, a lover?

"*Afaran*. Leave," he called over to the young boy who watched the falcon. The boy scampered off in the direction of the village.

The huge bird hung above them on a thermal updraught. The bird screamed as it recognized its owner below.

"He's beautiful," Cathy said. She shaded her eyes with her hand as she gazed skyward at the falcon.

The bird quivered as it stabilized itself in the air currents. It appeared to watch a movement far below in the meadow. Outside its warren entrance, a hare sat on its haunches with its long ears upright, either unaware of, or frozen with fear of, the falcon. Like a silent bullet, the falcon dove downwards, wings close to its body, aerodynamically sleek. With its vicious claws, it snatched the hare by the back of its neck. Screaming, the falcon flew to where Ed waited with an outstretched arm and dropped its prey on to the ground near Ed's braced spread legs as the huge bird landed on his bare arm.

Ed held onto the leather tethers on the bird's legs as he

picked up the dead hare by its hind legs.

"Time to return to the village," he announced, holding his right arm level with his chest as he carried the falcon.

Cathy remained several feet away, apprehensive of the ferocity of the falcon. Its beak, especially, scared her. *Looks like it would peck my eyes out.* She shuddered at the thought, picturing bloody, eyeless sockets.

"Tell me where you are from," he said.

Here goes, she thought. *Time to tell my story. Is he ready for this? Will he understand?*

He waited for her to continue.

"You may not believe me if I tell you."

"You are being very mysterious," he said quietly.

She stared him straight in the eyes. "I already told you. I'm from the future. Many hundreds of years from now."

He furrowed his brow and gazed at her with his pale blue eyes. "You ridicule me? I get muddled when you say the 'future.'"

Just as she feared, it appeared he couldn't grasp the concept.

"I have listened to a wise man at the next village, down the Roman Icknield Way," he continued. "He drew pictures in the sand to explain what this 'future' time means."

"And did you understand the theory?"

"I think I understand what is meant by 'future.' I do not know what you mean 'theory.'"

"It doesn't matter what it means, Ed. At least you're one of the few who have learned what future means."

"I understood what the wise man said, although I did not really believe what he taught. It is this way when I hear stories about the new god, Jesus."

"Let us keep these two subjects separate. Jesus is from the

past, while I am from the future."

"So how did you get here? Did you fly down from the sky? Is that where the future is? Are you sent from the gods?"

He sat down on a fallen tree by the side of the lane and rested his arm carrying the falcon on his knee. The falcon blinked and held its head to one side as it stared at Cathy's bare toes peeking out of her sandals.

She sat beside him, far enough from the falcon to make her feet feel safe, and looked into his cool-blue eyes.

"My husband and I were traveling in a car when it slid off the road. In the future, a car is a horseless cart. It has an engine which is made up of pulleys and little wheels and moves the cart along. We were both injured, and the next thing I knew, I arrived here."

He stared into her face.

"I am mystified. How did you travel back in time to my village?"

"I'm puzzled, too, Ed. I don't know how it happened. Sometimes I still think that this is a dream, or that I am dead."

"I do not believe it is so. You are not dead and how can this be a dream? I can touch your soft skin and can feel the sharpness of my falcon's claws. The earth is solid beneath my feet, and the wind blows your hair from your face."

Cathy rose to her feet, her forehead creased with concern—the whole situation puzzled her, too. They strolled back to the village. He guided her onto the correct footpath while he held the falcon away from her.

As they walked through the village, several men grinned knowingly at Ed. Younger women, clustered in groups, glared at Cathy. She, apparently, had stolen the one eligible bachelor left in the village—but had she? She hadn't decided whether to pursue him, or allow him to pursue her, or not.

Was she attracted to him because he resembled her husband? Maybe so. To remain a *spinster* would be lonely but endurable. Then she turned her head to look at Ed. *What a body. Rippling muscles in his arms and legs, washboard abs, long, blond hair, a thick neck. What woman could resist having such a body pressed against her?*

They arrived at Edith's house and stopped. She leaned over, avoiding the falcon, and on tiptoes, she kissed Ed on the cheek. "I had fun today."

"I shall see you at the wedding?" His eyes smoldered as he touched her face and gently ran a finger around her mouth. A shiver ran right through her body. She wondered if her toes would curl.

She swallowed hard to get her emotions under control. "Ethel's still angry with me because I didn't stay with Bega and learn to weave. She's ordered me to work the feast." She paused. "I hope to see you there."

"Until then…"

Cathy stepped into the house and closed the door as quickly as she could. She leaned on the panel and panted. *I have to decide what I'm going to do about this man sooner than I expected.* She threw herself onto her mattress. Her body tingled like a dizzy teenager.

"About time you returned!" screamed Ethel.

Cathy jumped up, terrified at the old woman's wrath.

"Get sweeping the floors in all of the houses." She shoved a reed broom into Cathy's hand and stormed out of the hut, mumbling something about lazy slaves.

Chapter 4

Time crept by and now it was a Monday morning five weeks after she'd arrived at the village. Cathy had slept soundly the previous night with the knowledge she had a long day ahead of her in the bake house. Ethel had told her how anxious she was to teach Cathy to cook and do the *bacan*—the baking—for the family and to take that chore from her. Also, the wedding feast would entail a huge amount of baking.

Cathy welcomed the assignment, and to be given the job was an honor. It meant she'd been forgiven for skipping out of Bega's weaving lesson, and now the family regarded her as a trusted slave. She looked forward to introducing some different recipes for tasty meals to the family. She surprised herself because she hadn't been at all domestic in her modern life. When she thought about it, though, she remembered she had cooked some gourmet meals when she and Al had entertained friends.

This job would keep her inside next to a warm fire in winter. As far as she could tell, it seemed to be the easiest job in the village. All of the other village endeavors involved heavy physical work. Yes, this cooking stint would suit her fine.

Ethel led her across the small compound to the bake house. The women stepped inside the thatched building. The interior consisted of a table and a huge clay oven in the middle of the floor

"This is an *ofn*," Ethel explained.

"It's still called an oven today," Cathy said.

The old woman ignored her. "My granddaughter has ground the wheat for us." She poured several pots full of wheat flour into a large wooden trencher. "Next, we add a little *gist*, yeast, which is a small portion of dough from my mix from yesterday."

She then handed Cathy a cup of water. "Add this a little at a time and when it forms a ball, start kneading the dough." She watched Cathy slowly adding the liquid while moving the dough around. "No, not that way. You have much to learn." She pulled the trencher away from her. "You have to— *beatan*—beat the dough."

Ethel sat down on a small stool and put one end of the trencher on the floor with the other end locked between her knees. With gnarled hands, she kneaded the large lump of dough from top to bottom of the trencher. "This is how you knead. Watch me because tomorrow, you will make the bread alone."

Both women then cut the dough into smaller pieces and rolled them into round loaves. These were covered with a cloth and left to rise.

Later, after the loaves had risen, Ethel said, "Now hit the loaves flat and knead them again. We will leave them to rise once more."

Once the loaves had risen the second time, Ethel opened the door of the oven using an old rag as an oven mitt. Using a long wooden paddle, she placed the loaves of bread on the bottom of the oven. She replaced the door with a satisfied slam.

"It will take very little time for the loaves to cook," she said with some self-satisfaction. "When the bread is done, I will add some juniper wood to make the oven hotter to cook the meat." Ethel turned a large, aged joint of beef to soak the other side of it in the garlic-laced vinegar marinade.

"Smells delicious," Cathy said as the garlic hit her nostrils. "Why juniper wood though?"

The old woman pointed up in the rafters at the bags holding smoked hams. "The juniper cooks the roast faster and the smoke gives the hams a good smoky taste. Different taste from hazel wood."

"Are you smoking the ducks and chickens, too?" Cathy pointed to the row of feathered poultry with legs tied together hanging on pegs on one wall.

"No, they are draining of blood." Ethel pointed to a pool of red fluid on the floor, which ran through the floorboards to the dirt hole beneath. "They'll be ready to bake in clay in the *ofn* later."

"I hope I don't have to pluck all of those feathers." Cathy wrinkled her nose. She hated plucking chickens. Tiny feathers crept up your nose and made you sneeze.

"Not this time. We will gut them and add sage under the skins. Then we cover and bake them in clay. Once they are cooked, we peel off the clay and the feathers come off with the clay."

"Sounds tasty."

"With a large mug of apple-wine or ale," the old woman added with a smile.

"Or meadowsweet mead," Cathy finished with a giggle.

Overall, Cathy had discovered the Anglo-Saxons ate fairly well, except in winter. The majority of meals were cooked in a cauldron over the open fire in the family's hall. One had no chance to be a finicky eater. You either ate what was provided you or went hungry.

Ethel poked the long-handled wooden paddle into the oven and pulled out a loaf of golden bread. She thumped the crust and made a satisfied, affirmative grunt.

"Here, make this *panne clæne*." The old woman shoved a used, dirty soapstone pan into Cathy's hands.

She scraped the stuck food off with a small bundle of twigs, then scrubbed it shiny using heather and sand mixed with ashes from the fireplace as a cleaner.

"The cloth has been hung across the roof of the hall, as you requested," Ethel said as she opened the oven door and removed the rest of the loaves of bread.

Cathy had insisted large pieces of fabric be suspended over the tables, cooking pots, and cauldrons. The thatched roof harbored birds, bats, black rats, and field mice. The animals' contaminated, disease-ridden droppings fell down all over the tables and into the cooking food.

"The droppings are full of evil elves with spears to make you all ill," Cathy had told the family members who'd been reluctant to comply.

What the heck, she'd thought without a guilty conscience. *I'll use any ploy to get them to cover up that filthy roof.*

"You have made other changes which help our family," Ethel said. "Many now believe you *are* from the future—that you are a wise woman." The old woman looked at her with a quizzical stare.

Cathy smiled and nodded. Some of the other changes she'd made were regarded as far-thinking on the level of a wise woman. The easiest change she'd made had been to insist everyone boil the dirty river water. The rate of illnesses had fallen dramatically.

Stories circulated around the village. She was a wise woman, the women whispered, because she had visions into the future and knew exactly what would happen to them and the village.

Most respected her and called her a *wicca*—wise woman—but many feared her and her so-called powers. Cathy made a mental note. They had to be watched. Some of these people could become dangerous.

Ethel banged a large spoon on the side of a large pan. The loud noise brought Cathy back from her daydream.

"As I said, you have made some sensible changes to our lives." She plopped the large joint of beef into the pan, along with a handful of onions and carrots. "Soon, you will not be regarded as a slave because of the changes you have made, and I think the head man will announce you to be the village wise woman."

"Do you believe that?" Cathy hoped so because to become a wise woman meant no menial work assignments.

Chapter 5

The rooster crowed loud and clear as though he were calling, "It's a nice, warm day." Weeks had crawled by. Cathy was losing hope of ever returning to her husband and her usual, modern life where everyone spoke modern English. She experienced periods of despondency and prayed that her life was just a dream from which she would awaken soon.

She pulled back the curtains hung between the large posts, crawled out of her bed, shook pieces of straw and heather off her clothes, and stretched her lean body in preparation for a busy day. She relieved herself over the hole in the woods and wiped with a soft mullein leaf. Then she washed with the smelly soap, scrubbed her teeth with a brush she'd fashioned from the frayed pith of a willow stick, and combed her hair. She slipped on fresh clothes that had dried on the clothesline and now smelled of crisp, country air.

The area around Ethel's family's houses bustled with men and women as they prepared for the wedding to be held that day. Every man, woman, and child had a specific job to perform, and they hurried between the main hall, the bake house and several other buildings carrying pitchers of drinks and trays of food.

Through listening to Ethel and some of the other gossipy women, Cathy learned about how the couple had gone through a handfasting ceremony a year ago. Colored ribbons had been tied on their joined hands by family members with a murmured spell, or a good wish for the couple.

Excitement sizzled in the air throughout the village. Huge pots of water had been heated for the bride to bathe in and to wash her hair. Her sister added precious, sweet-smelling oil to the water and splashed it onto her wedding garments.

Despite historical facts to the contrary, Cathy had been pleasantly surprised to learn all of the people in the village bathed every Saturday night and washed their hair. All except Ethel, that is, who complained she didn't have time to wash herself because she had to lug water around to everyone else.

Excuses, excuses. Doesn't she realize she smells?

She did, however, make an exception for the wedding.

Ethel appeared, her wrinkled face scrubbed shiny, with her hair combed and twisted into a bun on the back of her head. She wore a belt she called a *gyrdel,* from which several items were hung. One piece of metal, similar to a key, denoted her as the family's head woman. There were also the usual items—scissors, tweezers, ear-cleaner spoon, and a small knife, all clinked together as she walked.

A cruciform brooch had been pinned on her breast, with the long leg pointing upward. She looked almost attractive, but very officious, as she assisted in preparing the bride.

Ethel and the bride's sisters, as the maids, assisted the young woman, Annis, into her new wedding clothes. Her underdress, sewn from finely woven, pale green linen, had cuffs of the long sleeves fastened with silver engraved wrist clasps. One of the bridesmaids held the lilac-colored overdress above the bride's head and slipped it down the girl's slender body.

Amber brooches were pinned to the shoulders of her

cyrtel and a matching amber necklace hooked onto the brooches and hung across her chest. Her maids stepped back to admire the bride who spun around to show off her garments.

"You are beautiful," said her youngest sister.

Ethel pulled a pretty purple net cap and matching veil out of a pouch she carried.

"This will top off your lovely outfit," she said as she placed the cap over Annis's head and then loosely draped the veil over the girl's blonde hair. She clasped her craggy and calloused hands together as she smiled with satisfaction at the sight of the beautiful bride.

The maids giggled as they produced a circle of ivy and wild flowers and crowned the bride with the colorful wedding wreath. Annis blushed with joy as she wore the wreath like a sweet-smelling crown.

One maid sprinkled salt over Annis' wedding slippers. "To ward off evil spirits," she said. The bride sat down on a bench as the maid helped her into her shoes.

"The right one goes on first—for good luck. Then the left one with this special charm inside to bring prosperity."

Annis held a hand over her mouth as she stifled a sob. "I'm so happy. I think I'm going to cry."

Once ready, the bridal group walked in a procession snaking in and out of the houses, where family and neighbors stood and applauded with cheers. Garlands of flowers hung from the trees along the route. The young bride blushed, while her attendants strew flowers in her path and skipped to keep ahead of her.

They reached the forecourt area of the family's hall where the groom, Gerhardt, fidgeted nervously with his hands as he rocked back and forth.

The group leader, the *Weofodhegn*, stepped forward and announced that all had gathered there to celebrate the marriage of the couple. Cathy stood too far away to hear all of the prayers, but Ed soon found her in the crowd and whispered what the leader said into her ear. They were squashed together in the crowd with everyone craning their necks to watch the service. His hard body pressed against hers, which made her lose most of her concentration. It had been a long time since a man had been so intimately close. A few beads of sweat broke out on her forehead. She swiped them off.

"Now what's happening?" she asked. "I can't see a thing."

Ed leaned over. "The groom is giving the bride his ancestral sword to save for their sons. The bride is then to hand over a new sword to the groom to use to keep their home safe."

She blushed as she realized her breasts were crushed against his chest.

He looked into her face and grinned.

"You smell sweet," he whispered into her ear.

"Thank you," is all she could stammer.

The wedding couple made their oaths to each and the groom tendered his ring to the bride on the end of the new sword, along with the keys to his household.

Ed squeezed his body closer to her.

The leader announced the bride and groom now married and pronounced a blessing for the feast's food and wine. The crowd broke into cheers. The bashful bride looked up at the groom's handsome face. He leaned down and kissed her. Then, holding hands, with friends who sang and played a flat drum, a pan flute, and a wooden lyre, they led the way back to the main hall where the feast awaited them.

The crowd danced in circles to the music as the pure notes of the flute floated through the village. The beautiful strains of the music drifted through her head, bringing sad memories of her life with Al with them.

The buzz of voices emanated from the spacious main hall in the middle of the village square as women prepared the wedding feast. Wild flowers were scattered down the middle of the trestle tables, and more garlands suspended from the rafters.

The bowls and spoons were set out. A pile of pointed sticks were placed in the middle of the table to be used to pick up pieces of meat

Huge pots of mead, made from fermented honey, water, and yeast, along with apple wine, were lined up along the walls of the hall at the ready for the hot and thirsty guests. After she'd sampled a mug of the cider, Cathy felt dizzy.

"Whew. That is potent stuff," she said to Ethel. As she caught her breath, one of the young women shoved a tray of pottery mugs into Cathy's hands.

"Here, put one mug next to each bowl on the tables in the hall. Do not stand around while there is plenty of preparation work to be completed."

Cathy's knees bent under the weight of the heavy tray. She tightened up her arm muscles to heave the load of mugs as she made her way carefully into the main hall.

Teenage girls chatted as they moved around and filled the pitchers with either mead or cider. At last, the tables were ready.

Three large fire pits lined with stones had been dug outside near the main hall. One pit, filled with burning logs, had a spit on which a freshly-killed deer sizzled, while over another fire, a whole pig slowly roasted as it turned on a spit. Floured brown trout, caught in the river, fried in a huge iron pan with big, flat, mushrooms from the meadows. Green peas, onions, cabbages, and carrots boiled gently in a cauldron over the third fire pit.

The leader banged on a drum to get the crowd's attention.

"I hereby declare the wedding feast is ready," he announced. "Come, everyone, and enjoy."

The throng poured into the hall and found seats. Slices of meat carved off the pig and deer, along with pickles and vegetables, were consumed with gusto on the ends of knives, and thick wedges of fresh, buttered bread were washed down with ample mugs of mead, apple wine, and hard cider.

Soon, the inebriated celebrants were dancing in the aisles as more trays loaded with desserts were carried in on the young girls' shoulders. The trays were laden with sweet baked apple dumplings, strawberries smothered in cream, blackberries served with ladles of custard, and sloe plums sweetened with honey.

The party continued into the evening as the celebrants sat around the dying fires, singing, telling riddles, and playing games with the children. Cathy worked most of the evening clearing the feast tables and cleaning the cooking pots. At last, Edith permitted her to leave the work area and join Ed, where they shared a wooden bench and took part in the merriment.

Ed's leg rested against hers, which felt as though it would burn through the fabric of her gown. He circled his arm around her waist as they snuggled against the cool evening air, then leaned over, kissed her cheek and nuzzled his face into the side of her neck.

"I am glad you have been freed from your chores," he whispered.

"It's been a long day," she said with a yawn.

As the sun set, the bride and groom gave a signal, and with a crowd of well-wishers following them, which included Ed and Cathy, they walked to their new home. At their house, amongst cheers, the groom picked up the bride, carried her across the threshold, and with a backwards motion, kicked the door closed.

The cheering crowd dispersed, with some returning to the burning fire pits to continue the partying. Ed took her hand and pulled Cathy through some thick bushes into the shadows of a large oak tree. Cathy's heart skipped a beat and then fluttered as she landed in his bear hug. It had been a long time since she'd been manhandled. She needed that.

He released his arms from around her and turned her face up toward his. He traced her mouth with his fingers. He gently kissed her eyes and then his lips, now trembling, came down on hers, open and moist. With lips parted, his tongue sought hers. Her legs went weak as she reacted to his touch. Their hungry mouths responded in unison, seeking, plunging, and tasting each other.

She gasped for air as he slowly worked his way down from her trembling mouth to the nape of her neck. With deft fingers, he undid the brooches holding up her *cyrtel*. It fell to the ground. His hands cupped her breasts through her tunic. Then he carefully lowered her to the mossy ground.

Lying on the ground beside her, he cradled her in an embrace. She ran her hand slowly over his chest. Feeling a shudder ripple through his body, she traced lingering, small circles with her fingers over his abs and his stomach, ridged with taut muscles. He sucked in a gasp of air as he threaded his fingers through her hair.

"I want to take you now," he whispered.

Her body throbbed with anticipation.

"I am married to another," she answered.

"In another time. That time is not now. I want to be your husband and give you many babies."

He gently held her face in his hands. She turned and kissed his right hand, while her body trembled as she clung to him. Suddenly, Ed's body froze.

"Sssh." Ed jumped up and held out his hand to assist Cathy to her feet.

"What's wrong?" she said as she stood.

"I heard someone approaching." He stood behind her and wrapped her in his arms. They listened—holding their breath to hear without constraint.

"Cathy!" a woman's voice screamed through the darkness.

"There. I knew I had heard someone."

"Cathy! Where are you? We need your help."

"It's Bega." She disentangled herself from Ed's embrace. "Cathy!"

"Yes, Bega," Cathy called out. "Over here. Wait there."

"Hurry."

Cathy pulled up her *cyrtel* as she stepped through the shrubbery. She struggled with the brooches on her shoulders as she hurried over to where Bega stood. Tears poured down the girl's cheeks.

"What's the matter?"

"You must hurry. Ethel is very ill. She is writhing in her

bed. She is screaming in pain."

Ed stood by Cathy's side as she adjusted her clothing. She didn't care how unseemly she appeared. It was more important to get to Ethel. She'd become quite fond of the old woman despite her crotchety ways at times.

"What happened to her?"

"We do not know.. After the wedding feast, she said she felt ill. Just got worse. Please hurry," Bega pleaded.

"Yes, yes. Of course I'll go to Ethel. I hope I can remember what herbs I'll need."

Chapter 6

As she rushed to the old woman's bedside, Cathy recalled the day when Ethel had begun teaching her about herbal medicine.

"A wise woman is raised learning how to heal through herbs. You know nothing about herbs, so I shall attempt to teach you quickly," Ethel said.

Ethel picked up two willow baskets and handed one to Cathy. "For the herbs we pick. Follow me."

The two women walked side-by-side to the meadows and woods surrounding the village. Ethel explained the plants growing in the hedgerows and along the paths, giving her pupil their names and uses. Cathy made copious notes with a sliver of charcoal as her pencil on a shard of broken pottery as her notebook. She'd transcribe her notes onto a soft piece of deerskin with a quill and ink when she returned from the classes.

In the shade of the trees, Ethel pointed out bracken fern. "Only give a tiny amount of bracken to get rid of worms. Everyone has gut worms," she added. "Bracken is poisonous, so give only small amount."

Cathy underlined the warning words on her piece of pottery.

"A better herb for worms is *wermode*—wormwood—if you can find it. You can make a compress from it for bruises. When I have some plants, I throw some leaves on the floor of the living house to get rid of fleas."

Cathy scribbled her note.

"Mandrake is good for devil sickness, but the scream it makes when it is picked can kill you," she warned.

The woman is serious. Harry Potter, where are you? "So how do you pick it?" Cathy asked.

"We tie a dog to the plant and then we call it from a distance," Ethel said condescendingly.

"Of course. Whatever was I thinking?" Cathy shook her head as they searched for more herbs.

"Spagnum moss. Good for wound dressing." Ethel bent to pull up handfuls of the moss and placed them in her basket.

"Hawthorn." She pointed to the pink-and-white blossoms. "For heart problems. Over there, milk thistle for liver ailments. Boil the thistle roots with honey and it makes the person vomit. Over here is garlic. It makes a poultice for boils, or eaten to get rid of worms and cure infections."

Cathy quickly made notes and then busied herself as she collected the plant specimens and placed them in her basket.

"This is dandelion."

"Oh, I know what it does. It makes you pee the bed," Cathy exclaimed as she stated the modern childhood belief.

Ethel gave her a withering look. "It is for water swelling. You are correct."

She pointed to a daisy-like plant. "Chamomile for stomach upsets. Over here, eyebright for eye infections. There is feverfew for fever and headaches."

Cathy kept writing. "Slow down, Ethel. I can't write it all down when you go so fast."

"Time to return." The old woman looked weary.

"I have a basket full."

"We now have to hang it up to dry. When dried, we'll grind each up with a mortar and put it in a deerskin pouch."

"I can write the name of the contents on the pouch flap so I won't forget what's in there." Cathy felt like she had at least learned something new and sewing the pouches would keep her busy.

Ethel preceded her along the footpath back to the village. She hiked up her skirt to avoid getting it caught on the prickly thistles, but avoided the stinging nettles lining the path. She looked back over her shoulder as she continued with the lesson.

"When someone has oozing sores or boils, we bathe his body with vinegar and boil his clothes in vinegar also."

Disinfectant—known for centuries, Cathy internalized.

Ethel continued, "For deep wounds to the body, a strong onion soup is fed to the injured warrior. If we can smell onions through the wound, we know he is going to die soon."

"How awful."

"We then only keep him comfortable, but we do not waste any more medicine on that person."

Ethel took her out on many more excursions, teaching Cathy all of the herbal lore she knew.

Now Ethel lay in her bed of straw, moaning, holding her stomach, vomiting blood and what resembled brown coffee grounds.

"Looks like a bleeding gastric ulcer," Cathy announced to everyone crowding around her and the patient. "Please back up so she can get some air. I need room to move around, too."

Bega came running into the house, gasping for breath, and handed Cathy her large bag of herbs. "How is she?" she asked.

"Not good," Cathy answered, her brow knitted with concern.

The crowd went quiet. Some of the women whispered to each other as they huddled together in the shadows. A young man began playing a quiet melody on a pan flute. When she heard the music, tears welled up in Cathy's eyes as memories of the past came rushing into her whole being.

She wiped away the tears as she dumped the pouches of herbs from the bag onto the floor. She quickly found the pouch of chamomile and poured an amount into a wooden mug. She added boiling water from the kettle hanging over the open fire, stirring the herbs into the pale tea. She added some honey to cover up the bitterness.

One of Ethel's sons, Willhelm, put his arms around his mother's shoulders and raised her almost upright. Cathy held the mug of tea to her lips, and Ethel, although weak, sipped the hot liquid. She opened her eyes and smiled.

"Sip some more," Cathy whispered to her. "It will help your pain."

The old woman slept fitfully for the next two hours. Her family stayed crowded together in a corner of the living house—clinging to each other, fearful of the end of their loved, aged one.

Then Ethel stirred. Willhelm raised her up as Cathy once more touched the mug of tea to the old woman's lips. She took a sip.

"It is too late, dear daughter." She took a raspy breath. "You are freed as my slave. It is time for me to die. I am weary."

Cathy's eyes brimmed with tears. She had called her "daughter," a compliment from the head of this family. The old woman had been a gentle slave owner.

Ethel took a few more feeble sips of the tea before signaling she wished to lie down. Her son gently lowered her onto her bed. Her breathing became labored. As Cathy loaded the pouches of herbs back into her herbal bag, the old woman's breathing became shallower, and then the last, gurgling death breath rattled through her throat.

Ethel was dead. Her son lowered his head in sorrow. Hot tears ran down Cathy's cheeks. Her friend had gone. She felt more alone than ever.

* * * *

Daylight crept into the village that next sad day. Gentle hands wrapped Ethel's skinny body in a clean sheet of fabric and carried it aloft from the living house to the family's hall. There, loving hands bathed her in warm water scented with exotic oils and dressed her in clean clothes.

"She didn't have the patience to allow me to dress her hair in this way when she was alive," Hilda said as she coiled her mother's hair on the sides of her head. She smiled at Cathy. "So she's going on her last journey with pretty hair."

Then they placed Ethel's *gyrdel* around her waist. From it hung her earthly possessions of the key, her scissors, tweezers, ear-cleaner spoon, and her small knife. The women began to screech and wail.

The keening noise scared Cathy. Hilda took her arm and pulled her outside.

"It will stop soon and then we will bear Mother to her resting place, which is being readied now."

"It was such a shock, that is all." Cathy tried to make light of her reaction to the screaming. "We just cry quietly at funerals where I am from."

"My mother will be buried here at the village," Hilda continued, "next to my *fæder*—father."

Cathy suddenly felt homesick as she worried about her own mother. How was she handling her daughter's mysterious disappearance? *I miss you, Mum. I love you.*

The family members left the hall, following the funeral bier, which Willhelm and a nephew bore between them. They walked the pathways, weaving around the houses in the village as a farewell to its inhabitants. Respectful villagers stood silent, with their head coverings removed.

The procession arrived at the cemetery, which laid a fair distance from the houses. A man leaned on a shovel admiring the fresh, earthy hole he'd apparently just dug. He moved away to the edge of the cemetery as the crowd arrived at Ethel's burial site.

The men lowered the bier slowly to the ground next to the grave. Willhelm stepped forward. He carried a ceramic pot decorated with a horse on one side and put a small loaf of bread inside the pot.

Hilda placed her mother's pouch of herbs, the tools of her trade, next to the body.

"She has her herbs to enable her to be a healer in her afterlife."

A musician in the crowd plucked the strings of a lyre as he played a favorite song. Another played a mournful tune on a flute. Muffled sobs emanated from the women who gathered around as the men lowered Ethel into the earth. Her children threw handfuls of soil into the resting place and watched as the cemetery worker filled in the hole.

A large sled, loaded with large rocks, stood to one side of the cemetery. Two powerful men, both slaves belonging to the gravedigger, pulled it over to the burial place, then rolled the large rocks onto the mound.

"To keep away the wolves," Hilda whispered in Cathy's ear.

Cathy turned away and left with the grieving family and friends. Ethel had been the center of her life since she'd arrived at Stow. To whom could she turn now?

Just then, a big, rough hand reached through the crowd and touched hers. She strained to see who had touched her. Then she saw Ed with a somber face looking at her from the periphery of the group. She crossed the paths of others and finally reached Ed. She wanted some consolation.

"I'm glad you came," Cathy said. She held his hand tightly and pulled his arm close to her body.

They clung to each other as the crowd made their way to the family hall. It had turned cool, and Cathy pulled her shawl tighter around her shoulders. Ed put his arm around her in an attempt to warm her.

"The coldness is from the shock of losing Ethel. I feel like I've lost a family member."

* * * *

The fire had been stoked with logs that blazed cheerily with smoke pouring off the wood and circling the hall to escape through the door and windows. Ethel's family and friends had congregated around the fire.

"After a funeral, everyone gathers around the fire in the

family hall," Ed told her. "They remember the one who has passed into their afterlife, and regale each other with stories from the past."

"Sounds interesting," Cathy answered.

"Maybe you can tell us stories from your life?"

"They may find mine boring."

"I doubt you will bore me." He squeezed her shoulders. "I know, when I am an old man sitting around the fire, I shall tell my grandchildren about you and your stories."

"And where will I be? Not here with you and your grand-children?"

"I pray to the gods you are returned to your life. I must believe you will leave here and be happy back where you lived." He looked serious. "I would prefer you stay with me, but it would be selfish of me to want to keep you here."

The hall filled to overflowing. Benches had been pulled from the tables and set around the fire in a circle. Youngsters sat on the floor in front of the benches.

Alwin pulled in a small cart loaded with jugs of mead left over from the wedding. Bega and several of her cousins brought in trays laden down with bread and cheeses, cakes dripping with honey, and dumplings made from freshly-picked apples. They piled all of the food on two of the long tables alongside containers of cider.

Everyone clustered around the tables, picked up food and drink and carried it back to their places around the fire pit. Willhelm and Hilda began telling stories of their childhood, about how Ethel had been a loving mother, how hardworking she had been, and how much she would be missed.

Chapter 7

Cathy and Ed pulled a small bench to the back of the group, in the shadows thrown there by the burning logs. She squeezed close to him and ran her hand up and down his thigh. He reacted. His thigh muscles tightened as his right hand covered hers, trapping it on his leg. Inwardly, she groaned. It had been an immeasurable time since she had been satisfied by a man. Ed touched her face and turned it toward him. His lips found hers in the darkness. Her tongue ran over his soft lips as he gasped for a breath. Her body was on fire. She wanted to scream.

"Let us go outside," he whispered.

Cathy didn't answer, but stood up, and he tugged her by the hand around the crowd and out of the door into the darkness. He leaned back onto the wall and pulled Cathy against him. She moaned as his lips touched hers.

What am I doing? Hell, I'm not being unfaithful. This is another world, and a woman has needs.

His breathing accelerated. She touched his thigh. He held his breath as she made tiny circles with her hands, massaging his rigid muscles that ran into a tempting V down into his breeches. She straddled his leg and moved against it, pushing her pelvis against his. She could feel his hardness as his body sought release.

"Cathy, Cathy, Cathy, I love you," he groaned.

His wet lips sought her mouth.

"Cathy." A shrill voice vibrated in her ears. *Damn, Hilda crept up on us in the darkness.* "What do you think you are doing? Ed? Your lustful actions are outrageous."

The couple spun around to face the woman.

"How dare you spy on us?" Cathy snapped.

Hilda ignored her. "You should return to the meeting instead of cavorting outside like two youngsters. The family will be disappointed in you." She swung around and stalked back into the hall.

"Pay no attention to her," Cathy said as she and Ed clung onto to each other. Not moving. Then they kissed slowly and tenderly as they parted.

"I want you to be my wife," he whispered. "I love you. I am being selfish. I do not want you to return to your other life. I want you to stay here with me and be my wife."

"Do you really want a wife, or just someone to make love to?"

"I want both. I want you to be my wife and lover," he answered.

"I must think about this, Ed." Cathy hesitated.

If she decided to go ahead with the proposal, it would be a big move. Would she be a bigamist if she married him? She already had a husband, but she now lived in a different world from the one in which he existed. No, she needed Ed in her life. She needed someone to care about her, to work with side-by-side, to bear him children.

"Sleep on my question and we will discuss it in the morrow." He gathered her in his arms and bent to kiss her forehead. Holding hands, they rejoined the group in the hall and slipped back onto their bench. No one, other than Hilda, seemed to have missed them, although Willhelm stood up upon their arrival, as though he had been waiting for them. Facing them, he raised his hands to quiet the group. "Friends and family, please listen to what I have to say."

Everyone stopped whatever they were doing and turned to listen to him.

"Before Mother died, she told me if anything should happen to her, then, I, as head of the family, would have to announce the next wise woman."

He paused with his head lowered at the remembrance of her.

"She named the next wise woman who will have knowledge of the seasons, of crops, of the weather, and of all herbs to be used as medicine to aid our families."

He turned to face Cathy.

"The woman Mother named also appears to have knowledge from the future, although she has been unable to prove it to be true. This woman is named Cathy, but she will have to prove her claims before I will name her as wise woman."

Cathy stood as he announced her name. "Thank you, Willhelm," she said. "I'm flattered that your Mother considered me as your wise woman, but I do not believe I deserve that designation."

The crowd murmured and shook their heads in disagreement. It appeared they considered her to be their healer.

"Ethel taught me about herbal medicines. She was an able teacher and merely because I have knowledge of the future does not mean I have superior knowledge."

Another mumble traveled through the group.

"It only shows that, for some reason, I have come back in

time to this village."

Most faces in the gathering showed the fact their owners didn't comprehend what she said. *It would be a difficult point to get across,* Cathy thought.

"I will tell you about a death about to happen soon. Then it will prove I'm from the future."

Muttering moved through the group.

"King *Rædwald,* your High King of the Angles, will be buried at Sutton Hoo," Cathy continued.

Ed listened attentively as he watched her face.

"He was, or will be, buried with many grave-goods and provisions in a large ship equipped for his afterlife."

A gasp went through the crowd at the mention of the treasures.

"Along with him, there'll be a jeweled sword, beautiful gold jewelry, ingots of gold, glass drinking cups, gaming pieces, and spears."

"King Rædwald is alive and well, woman," called out one man.

"At the present time, yes, he is, but he will die soon, and he will have such a burial as I've described. His son, Earpwald, will become your king to whom Stow will pledge your allegiance. The new king will be a Christian and many people in the villages will also convert to the new religion."

She gazed down at the faces turned upward to her. "When this happens, it'll show you that I do have knowledge and am from the future. Until then, if I'm called upon, I'll use my herbs to heal your ills."

Cathy sat down. Ed took her hand in his, raised it to his lips, and kissed each finger.

"You are my wise woman," he whispered.

"Tell us about this new religion," yelled a middle-aged

woman pointing a work-roughened finger at Cathy.

"Yes, tell us about this man they called Jesus," another woman called out.

Cathy dreaded the question, "Who was Jesus?" Ed helped her step up on the bench again. She looked around at all of the inquiring faces turned to her.

"Christianity will be accepted by millions of people all over the world, but it's a difficult subject to explain," she said. "We only know the good deeds and miracles performed by Jesus by reading about them in the gospels written by his followers."

"So you know nothing much," sneered a young man. His remark caused a ripple of snickering to wave through the crowd.

"I am not the correct person to answer all of your questions."

"Then who is the person who has this knowledge?"

Several people who surrounded the truculent young man slapped him on his back, congratulating him. He grinned and nodded his head, positive he'd won the argument against this know-it-all woman.

Cathy wasn't about to get into an argument with him. Instead, she said, "There's a missionary setting up a mission which will be called a Christian church in the future. It's about a mile east of here."

"Pish. We have our own gods and goddesses. Why would we need another one?"

Many heads in the audience nodded in agreement to his question.

"What will happen to the gods we have now? We will be punished by evil elves and spirits for replacing them with this new god," an elderly man yelled from the back of the hall.

"You should go to the mission and listen to the monk

there."

At Cathy's suggestion, the crowd burst into noisy discussions.

Willhelm stepped forward. He raised his right hand to quiet everyone. He waited for the hubbub to stop. "What Cathy has said is true. I have heard of many people, from other villages nearby, who have moved to the place of the mission."

There were audible gasps from his listeners.

"The times are changing. Some villages are no longer. People are building new villages in new areas."

Wybert, the potter, stood up in the midst of the crowd. "'Tis true what he says. I will leave Stow and go to Ipswich in about one moon's time."

"Ipswich is now the center for pottery," Willhelm interjected.

"Yes, I will work with my cousin making wares we will peddle to the surrounding villages. My cousin has a revolving wheel to make the pots. I have to learn how to throw the clay on to the moving wheel." He laughed.

"We wish you well and much success." Willhelm offered his hand in friendship.

Cathy stifled a yawn. It had been a long exhausting day. Ed pulled at her sleeve and leaned over. "Let us leave now," he whispered.

They left the hall as inconspicuously as they could. They walked arm-in-arm through the village to her living house. There, they shared slow and burning kisses until she pulled herself away.

"Good night, Ed."

"Sleep well, my love. We will talk again tomorrow."

Chapter 8

The next day dawned with a rosy sunrise. *Red sky in the morning, shepherd's warning.* The old saying ran through Cathy's head as she brushed her teeth in the basin outside the family's living house. The sky didn't look like rain was imminent.

Even the usually rampaging children were quiet today. A shroud of sadness hung over the village as they mourned the death of Ethel. Despite being depressed herself, she still had to carry on her duties as the baker. So, after tying a length of fabric around her middle as an apron, she set out to walk to the bake house.

There she discovered a large barrel of flour sitting beside the table. Ethel's daughters, apparently up at the crack of dawn, had ground enough wheat into flour for the day's baking needs. Cathy sifted the flour into the wooden trencher through some loosely woven cloth to separate the ground flour from the weevils which typically inhabited all of the grains.

She made the bread dough, kneaded it, and set it aside to rise. Just as she walked toward the door to stand in the sunshine for a while, she heard a hello called from down the pathway. Her heart skipped a beat when she saw Ed walking toward her.

His blond hair glinted golden in the sunlight, and his arm muscles strained against the material of his shirt. He smiled as she stepped out of the doorway wiping her flour-covered hands on her apron. *Why does he have to look so much like Al?* She hadn't forgotten her husband, but in the past weeks, his memory had taken a backseat to her present situation, which took all of her waking hours to survive.

Life was hard in the village. She wasn't accustomed to as much manual work as she had to do right now, and she'd thought long and hard about making her life in this village more fulfilling. During the past few days, she'd mulled over her dilemma and had decided she needed to go on with her life—this life—and probably with a new husband. Of course, she hadn't told Ed of her decision.

Ed stepped in front of her and took her hands in his.

"They're covered with flour." She laughed.

He smiled as he pulled her hands up to his lips. "They are beautiful hands, belonging to the one I love."

"They're ugly and calloused." She pulled her hands away.

He frowned. "I must talk to you."

"Why so serious?" Cathy went back inside to check on the rising bread. Ed followed her.

Cathy dumped the pots of risen dough on the breadboard and began kneading the puffy lumps.

"Please stop working, Cathy. I have to discuss something with you."

Surprised by his demeanor, she quit kneading and faced him with anticipation.

"What is the problem, Ed?" She knew what he wanted to discuss, but feigned ignorance. *Am I ready for this? I believe I am.*

Ed stood with his feet apart, fidgeting, transferring his weight from one leg to the other and then back again. Nervous, he cleared his throat.

"I have been thinking a lot since the meeting last night. I only slept little. So many thoughts passed through my mind."

"Tell me what's on your mind, Ed?" She leaned back onto the wooden table.

He came over to her and took her into his arms. "You know I love you. I told you yesterday," he started, "but you never said if you love me." He looked like a little boy asking for a treat.

"I think I love you." She pulled herself out of his embrace and turned back to the chore of kneading the rising loaves. She pounded on a lump of dough on the breadboard. "But I'm not sure whether it's you I love, or if I love the fact you resemble my husband." Tears welled up into her eyes.

"I understand," he said quietly, almost pouting.

"I'm glad." She swung around to face him.

"Yes, I do understand. You are passing through a new life, but you carry with you the memories from your past life."

She stared at him. This hunk of a man had more intelligence than she had thought. "So what kept you up all night?"

"The stories told around the fire."

"About people moving around? Or about the new religion, Christianity?"

"About everything. I would like to travel to the new village near here."

"The one they will call West Stow in the future?"

"Yes, where the missionary is residing." He sounded enthusiastic.

"So you want to learn more?"

"Yes, and I want to see more of this new village and who is living there."

"And then what?"

"I am thinking we would move to the village and set up our own family—together as husband and wife...if you will have me as your husband, that is," he quickly added.

"Well, we have to see if this new place is feasible for us. When do you want to leave?" she asked as she piled more wood in the oven. She didn't answer his marriage proposal.

"As soon as you have finished your work in the bake house." He handed small logs to her from the high wood pile.

"I have to bake the bread for the family before I can leave," she said. She stood and wiped a bead of sweat off her forehead. "How are we going? Walking? It is not far."

"I wondered if you would like to go by cart? Two carts. I can teach you how to drive the horse."

"A cart will be fun as long, as you give me some instructions before we start out."

He smiled. "Good. I shall borrow the carts from my cousin and prepare the horses."

"Don't rush. I have to bake all of this bread before we can go." She didn't say anything to Ed, but she, too, was excited about visiting the new village. She was a free woman now and looked forward to exploring the area. Other than time spent with Ed, life had become a little stagnant at Stow.

* * * *

With the loaves of bread baked and loaded into large baskets, she combed her hair and smoothed her skirt before she hurried across the village to meet Ed.

Ed waited at the end of the grassy lane, where dirt tracks

were worn down by wooden cart wheels rolling their way down to the main road. He stood in front of the horses holding the reins of both.

He smiled as she approached. "You look fresh as a flower." He kissed her softly.

"Thank you, sire," Cathy said. She gave him a little bob of a curtsy.

"I will help you get into the cart." He held her right arm.

"It is a little difficult with a long skirt on," she called back over her shoulder as she hauled herself into the cart. She gathered the reins in her hands. "Okay, what's the next step?"

"Do not do anything yet," he yelled over to her. "To start, you have to shake the reins and click your tongue."

"I think the way to stop is the most important thing to learn first." It made her nervous to be behind this animal she had to control.

"You pull back on the reins, like this." He pulled back on the reins making his horse back up a few steps. "It also makes them back up when you are at a standstill," he continued.

"Is that all I have to know?"

"Yes, it is easy. To make the horse go faster, just shake the reins over its back."

He clucked his horse and started off at a walk down the lane. Cathy clicked her tongue and shook the reins over her horse's back. The animal moved forward quickly, and she clung onto the rail to save herself from falling out the back of the cart. Before long, she had control and felt at ease driving at an easy walk.

They turned off the narrow lane onto the wider road leading east toward the mission. The road could accommodate the carts side by side. Ed slowed his horse until she caught up to him. He looked over at her as they traveled down the road.

"You are doing well," he called over. "Would you like to go a little faster?"

"I think I could manage it," she yelled back. She slapped the reins on the back of her horse's back, and he began to trot. The wind rushed through her hair, whipping it loose from the pins, blowing it behind her. *Free—at last.* This was the first time she'd left the village since her arrival, and she felt as though she'd been released from a prison.

The air smelled fresh, clean, and warm, with no smoke from the smoldering fireplaces sneaking up her nose, making her sinuses hurt. Just clear air hit her face. She slapped the reins again. The horse changed its gait to a canter—as though it too felt free. Its mane blew in the wind as its legs moved with ease over the grassy road. She laughed out loud.

Ed in his cart thundered behind her as he tried to catch up with her. His horse put on more speed and drew ahead of Cathy's cart.

"I will soon catch up with you," she shouted.

Her horse gathered momentum as it ran at full speed, easily pulling the light cart and woman. Cathy felt the increased speed, but she wanted the animal to slow down now. As a little girl on a swing, she'd beg to be pushed higher, but once she did reach an enviable height, fear struck and she'd scream to get off. She'd enjoyed the ride in the cart and the race, but now the pace frightened her. She pulled back on the horse's reins. It slowed a little.

Panic set in. Her stomach lurched as fear gripped her whole body. *Please slow down. Please stop.*

The horse seemed set on running until it collapsed. "Ed," she screamed, "please help me! Get in front of my horse and slow him down."

Ed was too far ahead to hear her shriek for assistance.

The road bent to the right. Rocks littered both sides of the road. The cart pitched to the left as it approached the corner. She leaned her weight to the right as she pulled back on the reins. The animal slowed to a canter. Cathy breathed a sigh of relief as the pace slowed and she regained control.

A sudden movement in the hedgerow along the side of road caught her eye. *Oh, no, no. Not a second time. Can this be happening again?* The movement turned into a furry blur as a hare darted out of the hedge into the path of the cart. The horse squealed in fear, skidded to a halt and rose up on its rear haunches. The cart flipped over onto its side. Cathy grabbed onto the handrail, but the velocity of the flipped cart ripped her hand loose, and she pitched, headfirst, onto the rocks on the roadside.

The horse jerked as the shafts ripped lose from the harness, but the cart tipped over, dragging the animal down with it, rolling over onto its side. Then with a whinny, the horse raised itself up, first on its front legs and then the rear legs, and with a grazed and bleeding rump took off down the road. She saw the animal's exit through a haze of blood spurting from a wound on her head.

Just then, Cathy's horse ran by Ed. He pulled up on the reins of his horse and stopped it in the middle of the road. With shock showing on his face, he jumped out of the cart and ran down the road to where Cathy lay. She didn't move and blood ran down her face onto her clothes.

"Cathy—my darling." He moved her slowly onto her back. He tore off his shirt and ripped off some strips of fabric, which he used to dab her face. A long, open gash slashed across her forehead. "Cathy, Cathy." He tapped her face.

Cathy could hear his voice echoing around her head. *Ed, help me. Please help me.* Her pleas caught in her throat. Nothing would come out of her mouth. Helpless. Everything swirled around. Her head pounded from the gash on her head, and the whole world seemed to be swirling around. *Help me, Ed.* That was all she remembered as she sank into unconsciousness.

PART III

The Dragonfly

Chapter 1

Bury St. Edmunds 1606

"Young lady." He slapped her face gently. "Please wake up," he begged.

He and the driver had come across her as she stumbled along the side of the road and given her a ride into town. Now she'd tumbled off their cart.

"Ed?" she croaked as her eyelids fluttered but stayed closed.

"No. I'm Albert. What is your name?" He'd been shocked to see her fall off the dray. Her eyes remained closed.

There she lay, all crumpled up like a cloth doll, injured, her head bleeding profusely onto the cobblestone street. It began to drizzle rain, which mixed with her blood to create a stream of watery red running into the clay-clad gutter.

The huge shire horse stamped its metal-shod feet on the cobblestones. The clip, clopping echoed down the narrow driveway between the brick buildings. It backed up a little, which caused the dray, loaded with barrels of ale, to move closer to Cathy.

"Sorry aboit that," the elderly driver said as he wrapped

the reins around a metal hook on the cart. He climbed down off the dray clumsily because of his large girth. "Oi forgot there 'twas that big bump in the road. Should 'ave told 'er to 'old on," he said in the sing-song cadence of the Suffolk accent. "Cor, it do look loike a narsty cut on 'er 'ead." He wiped his brow with a scrunched-up, dirty, grey handkerchief he'd pulled out of his coat pocket. "Oi'll get someone from the 'ouse to 'elp us get 'er insoide." With that, he sniffed his beak-like nose, lumbered down the lane and entered one of the small back doors of the townhouse.

"Come on." Albert raised Cathy's head off the wet road. "Wake up for me."

* * * *

Her eyelids flickered open. "Al?"

He shook his head.

"You look like Ed and Al. What did you say your name is?" she slurred through swollen lips. The blood tasted like iron in her mouth. "Sorry, I'm confused. So you're Ed?"

"No. I told you. I am Albert. Albert White. I am not called Al or Ed," he snapped. "You *are* acting strangely."

She'd become conscious slowly. Things were still fuzzy, but were gradually clearing up, like warm breath disappearing from a cold pane of glass.

Where am I? And who the heck is this Albert? I want Al, or Ed, anyone other than another man. And this Albert looks exactly like them, and he has the same name as my husband. What's going on? I must be hallucinating.

"So, you say you're Albert?"

"I've told you my name twice."

She struggled up on her elbows, but the pain in her head shot through her scalp. She had to lie down again. "I'll call you

Alb for short," she said.

"Alb is what my Mother calls me," he answered.

"I'll call you Alb because I don't want to get you mixed up with someone else I know with the same name." *Forgive me, Al.*

"All right," Alb answered. "You have a strange way of joining your words together."

"Whatever do you mean?"

"You said 'I'll' instead of 'I will' and 'you're' for 'you are.'"

"Oh—you understand me, though, so don't worry about it." She ran her hands through her hair. "Where am I?"

"You are in Bury. Bury St. Edmunds."

"How on earth did I get here? I was on my way to West Stow—in a cart."

"You must have been daydreaming. You were stumbling along the road when we stopped to help you and put you in the cart. You fell out of it, too." He laughed.

Alb put his arms around her shoulders and pulled her up into a sitting position. The surroundings spun around as dizziness took over again. She raised her hand and touched her aching scalp. "Ouch. It really hurts."

Just then, a great flurry of activity broke out as an amplebosomed woman burst out of the house, followed by the cart driver. The woman wiped her hands on a soiled white apron as she ambled over to Cathy.

"Thank goodness you are here, Bessie," Alb called out to the approaching female.

"What happened to her?" Bessie asked as she leaned over and peered into Cathy's face. A grey, boned corset bound her trunk from the middle of her and then down to her hips. Her large, rounded breasts heaved up and down as she tried to catch her breath.

"She fell off the dray. I was hitching a ride back to the house on the cart, when we found her alongside the road. She is only wearing a night shift. I had gone to the market on the Cornhill to purchase some celery for Cook," he answered.

"What? Cook must be going a little barmy not remembering to put celery on our vegetable order. What is the world coming to?"

"Bessie."

"She could have made do without the damned celery," she gushed.

"Bessie Long. Enough!" Alb shouted. He handed the woman the celery. "I need help with this young lady. She is hurt. Forget about Cook. You do go on and on."

"Sorry, Master Albert. Forgot myself for a minute." She blushed as she took the clean end of her apron and wiped blood off Cathy's face. "You poor dear."

Cathy drew back. *If she spits on her apron and then wipes my face, I think I'll scream.*

"Are you the new scullery maid Cook hired?"

"I don't think I am. I don't remember," said Cathy as she held her aching head.

"You must be," Bessie declared.

"Driver, I need your help to carry this young mistress into the house," Alb said to the old man as he approached.

Just then, the upstairs window of a house across the lane flew open and a woman screeched, "*Gardez l'eau*"—*Gardy–loo*—*watch out for the water*—as she emptied the yellow urine out of a chamber pot into the lane. The driver moved quickly, stepping aside to avoid being splashed.

The old man bent down and took hold of Cathy's ankles, while Alb hooked his arms under her arms and raised her off the wet cobblestones. They carried her through the doorway, stepped into the kitchen and set Cathy down on a wooden chair.

"Master Albert, you had better get back to work before Mr. Derby finds you fussing around this young lady," said Bessie, a touch of urgency in her voice.

Cathy turned to Alb. "What work do you do? Who's Mr. Derby?"

Alb stood in front of her. "I am the first footman. Mr. Derby is the butler of this house. He is in charge of us all."

"A footman? What year is this?" Her head injury had left her befuddled. She'd arrived in what year this time?

"It is the Year of Our Lord 1606," Bessie answered as she cleaned Cathy's hair with a wad of soapy white rags.

"Good heavens, I can't believe I've gone into yet another time. At least I'm getting closer to home."

"I do not understand what you say," Alb said. He pulled on his singlet over his shirt and stood before her, transformed into a footman. He rubbed his heeled leather shoes on the back of his hose to polish the dust off. "You will have to explain what you mean by your remark one day, but now I must return to my duties before I am missed."

He donned a velvet peaked cap, and with a little salute to her, made his way up the stairs. He turned to look at her again.

"I have a terrible headache since I fell off the cart." Cathy wiped her hand over her forehead.

"No wonder," Bessie said, clucking her tongue.

"Would you please get me something for the pain?"

"I will get you some willow bark tea. Also make you a nice compress," Bessie said, while she bustled around, opening cupboard doors and looking for the medical supplies.

As Cathy sipped the herb tea, Bessie folded a length of brown butcher paper into a rectangle and then poured vinegar on it, soaking the wad of paper. Satisfied with the results, she slapped it on Cathy's forehead. The fumes from the vinegar soon cleared Cathy's sinuses and accompanying headache.

Jack and Jill went up the hill...

After a few minutes, Cathy said, "I feel a lot better, Bessie. Thanks."

"Good. Now you need some clothes. I will see if the parlor maids have some extra things you can wear. You could catch your death in that wet night shift."

Bessie soon returned, her chubby arms filled with garments. She instructed Cathy to dress in the darkened pantry.

Cathy held up the pieces of clothing to figure out how to wear them. She looked for underwear, but there was none to be found. She pulled the scratchy linen shift over her head, and it fell down to her ankles. She laced up the stiff, boned corset, which squished her breasts into two rounded mounds. The corset went down to a V on her stomach which made it impossible to bend from the waist. *Ouch!*

To complete the outfit, she donned a grey bodice laced up the front, a full skirt, and leather slip-on shoes. By then, she was sweating in the humid, dank pantry. She coiled her hair, still wet, under a little white cap and stepped into the kitchen.

"That's better," Bessie said with a nod of her head. "Well then, better get to work."

"You're going to have to tell me what I'm supposed to

do," Cathy whined as she pushed a stray lock of hair back under her cap. "The knock on my head made me forget everything."

"Tsk, tsk. Whatever next?" Bessie pulled a large saucepan off a nail on the kitchen wall.

She threw a big apron over to Cathy, who caught it and tied the strings behind her waist. *This will be interesting. Wonder what she'd say if I told her I was the baker in an Anglo-Saxon village?* She smiled at the thought. "And what does being a scullery maid mean?"

"It means you scrub all the dirty pots, pans, bowls, jugs, and whatever else we use while cooking the meals. You will be at the sink most of the day. You are the lowest staff member of the lower servants."

"Sounds ominous," Cathy joked. She'd started out as a slave at the Anglo-Saxon village, and she'd been able to overcome that stigma, so she'd survive this position in the household. *Have no other choice.*

"You will take in all the deliveries that come to the tradesman's door."

"Then what do I do with them?"

"You will take them to the proper places in the kitchen. Vegetables to the larder where it is cooler. When meat and fish are delivered, I will show you where to store them."

Cathy nodded.

"After lunch, I will have the housekeeper go through the list of your jobs. There are too many for me to tell you. Right now, I have to prepare the vegetables for lunch. You should start washing those pots in the sink." Bessie pointed, with a paring knife, to a huge sink in a dark corner of the kitchen. "Soap is in the cupboard."

"Very well." Cathy felt better with her headache gone.

So there she stood—a servant to be used up and discarded when too old—a scullery maid, the lowest of the low, in a house of a nobleman in town. *Who owned it?* she wondered.

"Bessie, who owns this house?"

"Why, Captain Bartholomew Gosnold, of course. You do not remember that?"

"I'd forgotten, I suppose," Cathy answered, although she did know about the captain. He had organized the 1607 journey to Jamestown, Virginia, where she'd just vacationed in the present time, and here she now lived in his house. It was all so confusing but exciting at the same time.

Cathy picked up a bucket of cold water and dumped it into the big stone sink. Another kettle boiled water over the open fire in the huge fireplace large enough to walk into the embers. She grimaced with the exertion as she carried the pot of hot water over to the sink and mixed it in with the cold water and soft soap she found in the cupboard.

After she'd scrubbed the breakfast dishes, she leaned on the sink to relieve her back, which throbbed from bending over the too-low sink.

"Get these saucepans, young lady. No shirking your duties."

"Sorry. Just resting my aching back."

Cathy wrestled the heavy metal saucepans over to the sink and sank them in the soapy water. *Darn it. I have to go to the toilet.* She crossed her legs and began to do a little dance.

"What are you doing now?" Bessie yelled over to her.

"I have to pee. Where's the commode, or do I have to use a chamber pot?"

"What? Oh, by-the-by, the captain does not allow us to empty pots out of the window."

"That's good to know." Cathy grinned.

Bessie ignored the sarcasm. "Go through the door over there." She pointed with the ladle in her hand. "It's at the end of the garden. Mullein is growing on the way there."

Cathy rushed over to the side door and trotted toward the small shed she assumed held the toilets. She pulled off some mullein leaves as she went by the plants. *So this is as far as humankind has come,* she thought. After a thousand years, the soft leaves of mullein were still the choice for toilet paper.

Once inside the toilet, the stench almost overcame her. She retched at the smell that assaulted her nose as she lifted the wooden lid off the hole in the bench. *Amazing—and this is how a noble's house is built.* She hated to think about the common people in the rest of the town and their toilet facilities— or no facilities more like it, because she'd seen feces in the gutter and urine running down the street.

Why am I even considering how the townspeople live? She wanted her old life back. *I want to go home.*

Chapter 2

Mrs. Andrews, the housekeeper, was a dour woman about forty years old with a pure-white face and shaved eyebrows. She wore a dark dress under a heavy corset that held her fat midriff like a round barrel. She had missing and rotten teeth and she smelled awful. A chatelaine hung on a chain around her large waist. On the chatelaine, keys to the household's doors and cupboards and small scissors hung and clinked together as she walked. The chatelaine reminded Cathy of the *gyrdel* Ethel used to wear.

The housekeeper quickly ran through the scullery maid's duties, so Cathy would be ready to perform her jobs the following day. She was informed that she'd rise at dawn when the bell on the church clock tower would ring and wake her. Then she would dress, and within a half-an-hour, have made her bed and be downstairs in the kitchen. There, she would stoke the fire, or reset it if it had gone out overnight.

Next, she had to empty all of the tin chamber pots of the female servants. She would be expected to assist the housemaids prepare breakfast for the upstairs servants who included the butler, the cook, the housekeeper, the footmen, and the ladies' maids. With those chores done, Cathy had to scrub the floors of the kitchen, the pantry, and the scullery before Cook arrived. Then the tables had to be set for the servants' breakfast, clear the dishes after the meal, and wash them as well.

Then it would be time to assist the lower cook, Bessie, in preparing the midday meal, all the time making sure the kitchen remained spotless. The list seemed endless and continued through the servants' and the family's dinners and evening suppers, until almost ten o'clock at night at which time she was permitted to go to bed. No one bathed, except for wiping off their faces, so Cathy decided to bathe with warm water in the kitchen sink before anyone else awakened.

A sick feeling shuddered through Cathy's body. She doubted she could survive this schedule, but had no other choice. She knew no one and had no relatives to take her into their care. In this world, a woman could only be married, work in a household, or be a prostitute. This would have to suffice for now.

* * * *

Cathy had dragged herself up the back stairs of the house to the maids' bedrooms only to discover, to her horror, she was to share a bed with another maid. The room had a single hard bed and pegs on the wall on which to hang clothes. The other maid was already in bed, fully dressed, snoring loudly, when she got there.

She'd wriggled out of her corset and scratched her midriff, which now itched from the painful bones poking into her flesh. *Now I know how the* Playboy *bunnies felt at the end of a day*.

Her bed companion snorted in response to Cathy's shove so she'd have room to lie down. Tomorrow was Saturday, and Cathy had been told she could have the afternoon off. She couldn't wait. Being exhausted from the day's work, she fell asleep immediately.

* * * *

A rooster woke her up when it crowed at the first light of dawn. At the same time, the bell rang in the church tower. Cathy slowly unwound herself from the knot she'd curled herself into to avoid touching the other maid, whose body stank. She brushed her hair and scrubbed her teeth with a corner of her apron. Today, she'd try to locate something to act as a toothbrush—a piece of pithy stick if she was lucky. Apparently, dentistry was in its infancy from what she'd determined by the people she'd seen with missing and rotten teeth. It appeared nothing much had happened in that area of expertise during the past thousand years.

She put on her corset, smoothed down the clothes she'd slept in and made her way down the wooden back stairs, treading softly so as not to wake the household. Once in the kitchen, she washed her face and hands at the sink, then scraped the ashes out of the open fireplace and placed kindling in the hot ashes. The kindling caught fire with sparks and snaps as it hit the hot embers. After she'd piled small split logs onto the burning kindling, she poured jugs of water into the large kettle hanging on the hook over the flames.

Cathy quickly swept the kitchen, larder, and pantry. She leaned the broom in the corner and tied an apron around her middle.

Bessie yawned and scratched her bosoms as she came down the stairs. She picked up a jug from the pantry and plunked it down on the table. "Want breakfast?" she demanded.

"I'm starved," Cathy said. "What's to eat?"

"Same as every other day, young lady. Brown bread and ale."

"Sounds wonderful." *I ate better in Stow.*

Bessie pulled a chair over to the table, scraping the legs on the brick floor. She hacked off a slice of bread from a large loaf, plopped it on to a tin plate, and handed it to Cathy. Then she poured out two mugs of ale, pushed one in front of Cathy, and slurped from her own. The lower cook pulled chunks of bread off the slice, speared a piece onto her knife and dipped it into her ale, then slopped it around in her mouth.

"Time to start breakfast," Bessie said as she heaved her weight off the chair. She took a large piece of pike out of the pantry and slapped it onto the table.

"What do you want me to do?"

"Have to cook some porridge and fish for the upper servants first," Bessie stated, reaching for a frying pan and small saucepan. "They have ale or perry—pear juice—today. So you go and get the drinks ready in jugs. Then beat up them eggs." She pointed with a spoon at a basket of eggs.

"And what is the family eating today?" Cathy asked when she came back to the table and put the heavy ceramic jug of pear juice on the table.

"Breakfast, they have bread, butter, eggs, honey, cold smoked ham, poached pike, ale, perry, and wine. The captain has cut down on his meals. He says he is becoming corpulent."

"Cut back? That amount of food and then they just sit around all day? We're expected to eat little and work hard?"

"We are servants and should not expect more," Bessie said with a sigh of resignation. "We are fortunate to receive free room and board as 'tis. Cannot complain, dear."

"Their dinner at midday is probably huge too."

"Usually a couple of fish courses, sausages, beef, mutton, vegetables, cheese, and fruit. We get to eat leftovers, if there are any. The captain is generous in that way. For dinner I have to help cook make pigeon pie as well as the other dishes. Company coming for dinner." Bessie sounded tired just talking about the meals.

"Goodness." Cathy wanted to say something stronger, but knew the speaking blasphemies carried heavy penalties. "So much food. I'd get fat eating like they do," Cathy said as she broke an egg on the side of a mixing bowl. Another eleven waited in a basket to be broken and whisked together. At least she had become used to cooking at Stow.

"Crush those egg shells," said Bessie. "Otherwise a witch will get hold of them."

"What would she do with them?"

"Stir 'em in boiling water—cause storms at sea, they do."

As Cathy whipped the eggs into a frothy, sunny yellow mixture, a large woman, whom she assumed to be the omnipotent cook, came clomping down the wooden stairs into the kitchen.

"This is Ursula. We call her 'Cook,'" Bessie said over her shoulder as she stirred the eggs in a frying pan over the fire.

"She soon will know me," Cook snapped.

"She does not remember anything—she lost her memory after she fell on her head yesterday," Bessie added.

"What a story." Cook threw some slivers of wood into the stove. "Albert told me that the second footman is in bed with a belly ache so he will need help. Meanwhile, go toast some bread. Here is the toasting fork." Cook pushed a long-handled wire fork across the table to Cathy.

Cathy's grandmother had toasted bread the old-fashioned way by holding it in front of the fire flames, so she didn't need to ask for instructions this time. Soon, enough toast had been made and she returned to the stove and the bubbling porridge and a frying pan full of fish.

Alb came down the stairs, buttoning his singlet.

"Is the family's breakfast ready?" he asked.

"Not yet. We're hurrying," snapped the cook. "The upper servants' meal must be served first."

"Just asking," Alb said.

"Take off your dirty apron, young lady," Cook called over to Cathy as she pushed a tray across the table. "Lend a hand to Albert and take up the food to the servants' dining room."

* * * *

The morning seemed to fly by. Cook and Bessie prepared pies, roasted meats, peeled potatoes, and more. The cleaning up of the breakfast pots and pans blended in with the scrubbing of the pots used for preparing the household's dinner. One meal seemed to overlap with the previous meal.

The second footman was still bedridden and so Cathy had to assist Alb with the family's dinner.

Alb grunted as he picked up a heavy tray of pigeon pies. Cathy heaved the second tray loaded with filled bowls onto her shoulder. She had worked as a waitress as a teenager, so she had the skills to carry heavy trays. *Who knew this would come in handy again?* She followed Alb up the stairs to the family's dining room, where she set the tray down on the serving dresser.

The long table was covered with a carpet. Alb took a white table cloth out of a dresser drawer, took one end of it by the hem and billowed it out over the table. Cathy caught the other end and smoothed it out over the carpet topper.

She and Alb transferred the dishes to the table. On a flat, square, wooden trencher, several small pigeon pies were artfully arranged with their tail feathers stuck into the top of the pastry. A baked carp stared up with opaque eyes from an oval baking dish, and a mutton roast rested on a wooden cutting board.

"The Captain and Mrs. Gosnold prefer pewter," Alb said as he placed pewter mugs at four place settings of small plates. "Two guests are dining here today."

A Delft salt cellar sat in the middle of the table. Large napkins were placed next to the spoons, two-tined forks, and knives.

"I haven't seen forks like these before," Cathy said as she picked up one of the small forks.

"Only rich people use them."

"So what do we commoners use?"

"Spoons or our fingers, of course." He looked at her in amazement. She could tell by his expression he was wondering if she was a dullard.

"Don't your hands get disgusting, covered with food?" She lined up the cutlery neatly beside each plate.

"That is what the napkin over your shoulder is for, to wipe your hands." He held the empty trays up to his chest and stared at her. "Where *are* you from? Are you a foreigner? You seem not to know anything."

"It's a long story." Cathy stepped away from the table and walked toward the door. "Now is not the time to tell it either."

"You promise to tell me more—soon?" He clomped down the stairs behind her.

"Maybe."

They reached the kitchen. "Would you like to go down to the River Lark this afternoon?" he asked in a stage whisper.

Bessie overheard him and grinned. "Oh, dear. Seems like he has taken a fancy to you. Going to walk hand-in-hand down by the river," she teased.

"We are just friends," Alb said.

"Who are just friends?" a young woman asked as she came down the kitchen stairs.

"Cathy and I," Alb answered with a blush.

"What?" The young woman scowled. "I thought I am your favorite."

"This is Jane Marsden, the nursemaid," Alb said to Cathy.

"What can we do for you today, Mistress Jane?" Bessie asked.

"I have come to see why the children's dinner is late," she demanded.

"The reason is the second footman is ill."

"That is not a good excuse," Jane snapped. "The children are irritable because they are hungry."

Jane seemed better dressed than the rest of the servants. She wore a faded, worn dress with puffy sleeves and a lace collar.

"I like you in that goose-turd dress," Bessie flattered her, with a smile.

Cathy assumed "goose-turd" referred to the color of yellowish-green. She also assumed that the dress was a hand-me-down from the lady of the house because it had become a little shabby and was slightly too big for the slender frame of the nursemaid.

Jane flounced around the kitchen, giving sideway glances at the handsome footman. She picked up a stick of celery and waved it around as she spoke. "What are your plans for this afternoon, Albert?"

"I'm going out to the park for some fresh air."

"With this *scullery* maid?" She pointed to Cathy with the celery and looked her up and down with disdain.

"You do not have to be rude, Mistress Jane," Alb scolded.

"You will not speak to me in that fashion, Master Albert," Jane spat back. "Maybe I need to report your behavior to the captain." She narrowed her eyes.

"It will not be necessary. I apologize for my words," Alb said quietly.

"Good." She turned on her heel and began to climb the stairs. She turned as she said, "Bring up the children's dinner immediately."

Cook clucked her tongue. "Well, I never. Such goings on."

"I'll carry up the children's dinner," Cathy volunteered. She wiped off one of the trays she and Alb had just brought downstairs.

"There is no need. The nursery is all the way up on the third floor," Alb said.

Ursula loaded the tray with dishes of food.

"How many children are there?" Cathy asked.

"There are five—Robert, Susan, Bartholomew Jr., Paul, and Mary," Alb said.

"They lost two little darlings. Martha and Francisca. Such a pity," Bessie added. "It was ever so sad when they died. The captain named an island after Martha. Martha's Vineland in the new country."

"I've heard of that place," Cathy added before she could stop herself. *Don't draw attention to yourself.*

With the tray up on her shoulders, she made her way up three sets of winding stairs to the nursery. She panted to catch her breath when she reached the hallway with a door open to show a child's room. She took this to be the nursery and entered.

Jane sat on a stool as she brushed a little girl's hair. Two little boys played marbles on the bare wooden, plank floor.

"Put it down there on the table," Jane commanded. "I shall ring my bell when we are finished, and you will then come up and clear the table."

Cathy bobbed a quick curtsy and left the nursery.

As she returned to the kitchen, she looked forward to the afternoon ahead of her away from the smoky fireplace and greasy water in the sink. The weather promised to be warm and inviting, and the fresh air would clear away any clouds that still lingered in her head.

Why am I here? I'd become accustomed to my life at the Anglo-Saxon village. Ed had asked me to marry him, and now he's gone out my life forever. God, if you're up there, please get me back to Ed—or my husband, she added quickly.

Chapter 3

The afternoon arrived with warm breezes. Alb had changed from his formal footman's uniform and wore a puffy-sleeved shirt and breeches. Cathy wore the clean skirt she'd found on the peg in her room and she'd picked up a small basket from the pantry as she walked by the door.

He met her in the courtyard and they went through a passageway between the buildings and out onto the street in front of the brick manor.

"Let us go up to Cook's Row first," Alb said, walking backwards in front of her. "We can purchase a gloriously delicious sweet pastry, then carry it down to the river, where we can devour it without conscience."

"And pray tell me, where is this Cook's Row?"

"It is the street leading down the hill to the Abbey Gate."

"Oh, I think I know where it is. It's called Abbeygate Street several hundreds of years from now," she said.

"What do you mean by 'several years from now'?" Alb asked, almost under his breath. "Do you see the future?" He looked around to see if anyone overheard him.

"I am *from* the future," Cathy burst out. She wasn't going to hide her past in this period of her life. She didn't care; she wanted to get it over and done with. Alb looked like an intelligent man. He resembled Al and Ed, so why wouldn't he be intelligent, too? She was past worrying about things.

"Ssh." Alb held his finger up to his mouth. "You must not say that. To see the future is considered witchcraft."

"At this point, I don't give a goddamn." The swear word had slipped out before she could stop it.

"Cathy, a person could have their tongue cut out for swearing about God. You must be more careful," he muttered as he grabbed her arm and pulled her close to him.

They had walked almost up to the Abbey Gate.

"Let us cross over the street." Alb steered her in that direction. "Poor people wait around the gate to beg for bread. They're filthy dirty and have lice."

"What a shame." Her leather-soled shoes slipped on the rounded cobblestones in the street. Alb grabbed her around the waist to save her from falling. She could feel his firm body as he touched her.

"Thanks, Alb," she said as she leaned against his chest.

They continued up the street toward the Angel Hotel. It appeared to be a coaching inn. In the present time, it was still a hotel. *If only those walls could talk,* she thought.

"Alb, you're a servant. Don't you think of yourself as a poor person?"

"Absolutely not. I am a footman in a gentleman's home, which is a great honor." He sounded insulted. "I am a distant relative of the captain, thus I am not considered poor, as you call it."

"I didn't mean to upset you," Cathy said quickly.

"No offense taken. We are related, with some land to farm, but my family is not as well off as the captain, of course."

"Interesting."

They walked uphill along the Cook's Row lined with small shops and stopped in front of one establishment with a small glass window. They could see the interior of the shop through the open door. Bunches of herbs hung on strings from the black ceiling beams, while jars of spices lined the shelves. The shopkeeper, in a large grey apron over a full-sleeved shirt and knickers, assisted townswomen in choosing spices and herbs for their recipes. He folded their choices into paper envelopes.

"The baker's shop is just up the street," said Alb.

"Good. I'm getting hungry. I'm not used to having such a huge breakfast of bread and ale."

Alb laughed at her remark.

"You can laugh, but as one of the upper servants, you ate a decent meal. I'm really hungry."

The couple made their way up the street, passing houses and shops built in the half-timbered style that hung over the walkway. "Shops occupy the downstairs as you can see," Alb said, "while the owner lives upstairs."

"Many of the houses like these are still standing in town here in the twenty-first century," she told him.

He raised an eyebrow as though he wanted to question her further, but said nothing. They entered a warm shop with a sign over the door reading, Smith, Baker of Pies and Bread. The establishment smelled like baked bread. Cathy's nose took in the delicious aroma as she reminisced inside about her past days of baking bread at the village.

Crusty loaves of bread of all shapes and sizes spilled out of large square baskets lined up on a low shelf, while apple and peach pies emanated fruity smells, mixing mince with apples, with cherries, with rhubarb. Cathy's stomach growled with hunger, overwhelmed by the mouth-watering smells of the tiny shop and its fare.

Alb had some coins in his pocket. She had none.

"Put your coins in that bowl," said the baker as he pointed to a brown bowl of vinegar. "No plague-ridden money in my establishment," he added as he fished out two small coins as change.

After he'd been paid for the long loaf of crispy-crusted bread and two small cherry pies, the baker carefully laid the pies and bread into her basket to avoid breakage. Cathy covered them with the tea towel lining the basket.

Alb carried the basket as they continued along Cook's Row as far as the market square. Whole families, in town from the country, dressed in their best clothes, paraded around as they shopped in the little stores.

Standing in the market place, a group of street entertainers included three musicians and two men juggling clubs. One musician banged on a handheld drum, one played a flute, and another played a mandolin-type instrument. The flute echoed in her ears, and it brought back a flood of memories of Al and Ed. Tears brimmed in her eyes.

"This is always busy on market days," Alb said. He waved his right hand around the square. Facing the Moyses Hall, he pointed to his left and described it as the corn market, with the butter and cheese market on the right-hand side.

"This place will still be named the Cornhill and the Buttermarket in years to come," she said. She wished she were in the future right then. Tears ran down her cheeks and she was glad Alb looked away and not at her.

The couple strolled the downhill street toward the great Abbey Gate.

"The visitors at the manor house this evening are members of the Virginia Company," Alb said. "One of the gentlemen is Edward Maria Wingfield. They are here to discuss the journey to the New World to establish a settlement. They've secured a charter from the king."

"I've heard about that settlement," Cathy said. She tried to sound disinterested and not so much of a know-it-all, which seemed to annoy Alb.

"My cousin, William White, has already volunteered to accompany Captain Gosnold. Although he will merely act as a laborer, he believes it will be an adventure that should not be missed."

"It's going to be a dangerous expedition."

Alb paid no attention to her.

"They are to look for gold and the water route to the Orient," he continued.

"They won't find either." *Bite your tongue,* she told herself.

Again he ignored her.

"The captain and the other members of the company are leaving in two days for a meeting about the expedition."

"Where to?"

"To the captain's family seat, Otley Hall, near Ipswich."

"*Gipeswic* in Anglo-Saxon."

"I beg your pardon?"

"Sorry, Alb. Ignore my silly remarks."

He shifted the basket to his other hand. "Hand cramped up," he explained. "Anyway, as I was saying, my cousin has volunteered and I want to volunteer also. The gentlemen on the voyage will need a footman."

"That's ridiculous," Cathy snapped. "The living on a ship may require some help to the gentlemen, but once in Virginia, they'll need laborers, not a footman."

"Why do you say such a thing?"

"I've told you. I'm from the future and I know history."

"You owe me an explanation of how you arrived here, and what you know about the future."

"Once we get down by the river, we'll sit and have our picnic. I'll tell you anything your heart desires."

"Agreed." With a big grin, he took her hand and both jogged through the grounds of the old Abbey. They slowed down to a casual walk after Cathy complained of blisters on her feet from her ill-fitting shoes.

"What do you do for fun?" Cathy asked to divert the conversation to another subject for the moment.

"My cousins at the house are too young to play games with me, but when I have a day off, I sometimes play dicing with other servants. We meet at a house in Hatter Street. No gambling, of course."

"Of course not." Cathy laughed at him.

"We would lose our jobs if we were caught gambling. It is not a laughable matter," he said curtly, as he showed some irritation at her mockery of him.

"At times, when the family stays at Otley Hall, I am released from my duties for a fortnight or so. Then I return home, and I and my brothers will take our falcons out for some hunting."

"Sounds like fun. I had a friend who practiced falconry."

"Really? Would I know him?"

"No, he's history now."

"What? Your speech is so strange."

"That's part of my story. You'll have to wait until we've eaten our bread and pies, and then I'll tell you." Her stomach growled at this point. The breakfast of dry bread and ale failed to keep away the hunger pains.

The quacking of ducks greeted them as they arrived at the river with the Monk's Bridge to their left. The River Lark flowed through the three rounded arches of the bridge, while willow trees gracefully bowed leafy tendrils of branches over the river banks. Dragonflies dipped and touched the water surface as they danced in the sunshine.

They found a level spot of grass and set down the basket. Cathy spread out the tea towel as a tiny tablecloth. She broke off two chunks of the fresh bread and handed one piece to Alb. There they dined on the crusty bread and the little cherry pies, still warm from the baker's oven.

"Alb, if I tell you what I know about this journey to Virginia, will you reconsider your plans to go with the captain?"

"I have no idea, until I hear what you have to tell me." He shifted his weight onto his arms as he stretched out on the grass.

"I don't want to dissuade you, but I do have knowledge about the fate of those who went—or rather, will go—on this expedition." She hoped he would change his mind about going with Gosnold. It would be a shame to waste this handsome, intelligent man on some ill-fated journey to Virginia.

"So tell me your story—all of it. I'm curious to know every little detail," he said.

"All right. Here goes," she said.

She began with the car accident by explaining a "car" as a horseless carriage with a motor that moves the vehicle along the road. Childlike, he stared at her in amazement.

"What a wonderful world it will be with such a contraption," he murmured. He clearly didn't want to interrupt her wondrous tale.

"So, after the accident, I woke up in an Anglo-Saxon village. The people were friendly and they worked hard. A woman taught me how to make bread, and how to gather and cure illnesses with herbs. Because I knew so much from the future, they had begun to think of me as the wise woman. I met a man at the village, a blacksmith, and we fell in love. He wanted to learn more about Christianity and so we were on our way to the West Stow mission to learn more from the missionary who lived there."

"Why did he want to learn about Christianity? Were they not Christians already?" he asked.

"No. They were pagans back then. They worshipped many gods, but missionaries were spreading the gospel of Christ, and more of the Britons were converting to Christianity."

"How interesting."

"Well, on the way to the mission at West Stow, I was thrown out of my horse cart and hit my head. Then you know the rest...I woke up on the road near Captain Gosnold's house."

"Ye gads, what a story," he exclaimed. "And you swear it is true?"

"Yes, I swear it's true. Why would I make up some insane story if it weren't true?"

"Do you remember everything from the future?"

"Yes, and I also remember the history that I studied at the university."

"Captain Gosnold attended Cambridge University," Alb

said.

"Yes, I know. Then he went on to become a lawyer, but preferred to have adventures on long sea adventures."

"And he is about to go on another voyage," Alb added, with passion in his voice. He threw some small chunks of bread to the ducks in the river. Quacks and splashes ensued as the flock of water fowls fought over the treats.

"I could tell you how the expedition fared," Cathy said. She brushed some crumbs off her skirt as she got up off the ground.

"I am not sure if I would like to hear about its fate."

She felt the fabric in her skirt. "This grass is wet. Let's go over there and sit on the bench near the ruins," she said, pointing to a pillar of flint rocks that used to be part of the cloisters.

He dragged his heavy boots through the grass, freshly clipped by a group of sheep now chewing on the lawn on the other side of the abbey grounds. Cathy brushed some bench dust off the seat and then sat down.

"That's more comfortable," she said. "The grass is damp. My grandmother would swear I'd come down with piles from sitting on dampness like that."

Alb smiled at her. "And it will not?"

"No. It's an old wives' tale. You don't believe it do you?"

"Absolutely not. You keep changing the subject, Cathy," he said accusingly. "Get on with your account of Captain Gosnold's voyage."

"Sorry. I guess I'm avoiding it and anticipating your reaction," she answered.

He turned and put one leg on the bench in order to face her. "It seems you are avoiding telling me your story of the expedition."

"Not any more," she said, and began to tell him the history of the Jamestown settlement.

"The captain's backers financed the expedition to Virginia. They planned it at Otley Hall, his family seat, and set sail from Blackwall on the Thames River. He captained the *Godspeed*. Other ships on the journey were the *Susan Constant* and the *Discovery*. Storms delayed their departure, but they finally arrived in May at an area in Virginia on the James River, and named it Jamestown. It appeared more secure from the guns of the Spanish ships." She stopped to recall the remainder of the story.

"Sounds like a great adventure so far—something I would like." Alb urged her on.

"Ah, but then reality set in at Jamestown," she said. "The local tribe of Indians attacked the group, forcing them to build a fort, triangular-shaped, to protect themselves."

"How do you know about their fort?" Alb asked.

"A group of scientists have just discovered it. Or rather, in the future where I'm from, the remains have been discovered."

"Go on with the story."

"Well, to cut a long story short, the majority of the men died by autumn of the wounds from being attacked, dysentery, and typhoid fever from the dirty swamp water they drank."

They were silent for a moment.

"Will my cousin perish?" Alb asked with a worried look.

"I don't know if he lives or dies. We do know, from the accounts written by Captain John Smith, that Captain Gosnold died on August 22nd and was buried with great honors. He was only thirty-six."

"How do they know, for sure, that the captain died? Captain Smith may have imagined up that story."

"The scientists have found a skeleton they presume is Captain Gosnold by the articles buried with him. Plus, in the future they can test and compare one person to another person to see if they're related." She avoided mentioning DNA testing since it would be far too complicated to explain to this medieval man. "They'll compare it with living descendants of the Gosnold family and, yes, he really did die at Jamestown."

"I should warn all of them," Alb exclaimed.

"No, you can't warn them," Cathy said emphatically. "They would want to know how you knew this, and you'd look pretty silly explaining to them that I told you, and I know what's going to happen to them because I am from the future. No, there's nothing you can do, except not sign up for the voyage with your cousin, to save yourself from a certain death."

"You do not know if my cousin became ill or survived, so why should I not go on this voyage? I could also survive."

She sighed. "Then do as you want, Alb." She had resigned herself to the fact she probably had made no good argument against him going. She stood up, straightened her skirt, and picked up the empty basket. "Time to get back to the house. I have to wash all the dinner dishes and help with cooking supper."

"The afternoon passed so quickly. It has been very pleasant," said Alb. "I have heard so much."

"Yes, but did you learn anything?"

"I certainly did," he answered. "I thank you for your frankness." He took her hand and hooked it into the crook of his arm, and they laughed and joked for most of the way back to the manor house.

Before they arrived, Alb disengaged their arms.

"It is frowned upon for servants to be seen so familiar in public," he explained.

"Thanks for the tip," Cathy said with a smile. She opened the kitchen door and stepped down onto the brick floor.

"About time you returned to your work," greeted her, before her eyes had a chance to adjust to the darkness of the kitchen. Jane stood there, arms akimbo, at the bottom of the stairs.

Chapter 4

"So, why are you late?" Jane demanded.

"I am *not* late. Who are you to boss me around?" Cathy said, her anger flaring.

Alb stepped up behind Cathy, put his hands around her waist, and moved her aside. "Now, ladies, let us not be unpleasant to each other."

Cook just looked askance at the trio as she continued to beat a cake batter. Bessie tried to hide a slight smirk, but not successfully, while she sliced carrots into a large saucepan.

"We have had an enjoyable afternoon down at the river side," Alb continued. He had taken his singlet off the peg in a back room, donned it quickly, and turned into a footman once more. "Cathy told me about her life."

Cathy frowned at him as she attempted to stop him from telling the nursemaid about their conversation.

"That must have been enthralling," Jane spat out.

"In fact, it is fascinating. She is a woman who has succeeded, despite many adversities she had been forced to endure."

"Really?" Jane walked over to the big wooden table, pulled out a chair, and sat down. Absentmindedly, she picked up some pea pods and began to shell the peas into a bowl. "Do tell me what this scullery maid has overcome in her lengthy lifetime."

Cathy caught Alb's eye. She gestured for him to stop talking about her. He stopped himself before blurting out more information.

"I do not have time right now," he said, avoiding meeting Jane's stare. "I have to see if the captain needs anything."

"Your little scullery maid seems to have attached herself to you like a slimy leech, Master Albert," Jane said in a sarcastic, sing-song voice.

"I do not like your tone, Mistress Jane," Alb responded. "It is of no consequence to you whether she has attracted my attention or not."

"Ah, but it is, kind sir, if it causes you to shirk your duties."

"It will not affect my duties, Mistress Jane. Should I interpret your reactions to my friendship with Mistress Cathy as jealousy on your part?"

"Absolutely not." Jane jumped up, knocking the bowl of peas over onto the table. "What insolence to suggest such a thing. You are a mere servant, and she is nothing but a lowly scullery maid."

"She is more than you suspect. She has gifts of seeing into the future. She knows the fate of the captain's expedition. A talent to which you cannot aspire," he blurted out.

"Oh, really? She can see the future?" Jane sneered. "What has she told you?" She crossed the kitchen and faced Alb, blocking his escape to the stairway.

"Nothing."

"I do not believe you. What has she told you? That gold will be discovered in the New World?" she goaded.

"The exact opposite," he said. "She told me that the expedition is ill-fated and most of them will die, including the captain."

Now what? Cathy wondered.

He turned to look at Cathy.

"Jane," Cathy said with a smarmy smile, "surely you don't believe that?" She turned to Alb. "Tell Jane you were just teasing her." She glared at him.

"Um…yes…that is right. I am just teasing you," Alb stuttered.

"I do *not* believe either of you," Jane said. "I shall mention this to the captain." She turned on her heel and quickly ran upstairs.

"You've done it now," Cathy hissed as she poked a finger in Alb's chest. "Are you out of your mind? Jane could cause us both a lot of trouble."

"I am sorry for my outburst," he said. "She angered me. I will go upstairs to the nursery and try to dissuade her from telling the captain."

"You should go up—now." Cathy's chest tightened with fear. That woman could be her downfall during this superstitious time in history.

"I fail to understand. If what you said is true, why should I tell Jane it is not true?"

"You really are a naïve…no…stupid man," she snapped. She pulled him aside, away from Bessie and Cook, who had already heard too much. "What I told you *is* true, but she'll twist it so I'm made to look like a fortuneteller, or worse."

He stamped up the stairs and disappeared through the door at the top of the landing.

Cathy went over to the sink and poured some hot water

into it to soak the dishes piled up, waiting to be washed. She added soap and began scrubbing the plates.

Bessie broke the silence as she shelled peas into a colander. "Jane could cause a lot of problems for you, you know."

"Her uncle is a judge in the county," Cook added.

"What do you mean?" Cathy said as she scrubbed a greasy plate.

"It means she has strong connections to important and dangerous men," Bessie explained.

"Why 'dangerous'? I haven't done anything wrong," Cathy asked with phony innocence. She was well aware of the meaning of the woman's threats, but felt compelled to act like she didn't understand the consequences in front of the other servants.

"We will wait and see," Cook said. "Meanwhile, finish those dishes and then scrub these saucepans. When you've done with those, help Bessie with the vegetables. We are running behind time."

Cathy determined that each woman had said all she was about to divulge and did not wish to expound on the meaning of their remarks. She had a sick feeling in the pit of her stomach. *Ed. Al. Help me out of this situation.*

That evening Cathy kept up with all of the dirty pots and pans, and helped with the food for dinner. She noticed Bessie, Cook, and the other lower-level servants and maids who entered or worked in the kitchen were especially quiet. They gathered in little groups, whispering, darting looks in her direction, and avoiding contact with her. She wondered what they were discussing. The women were obviously afraid to talk to her.

They're talking about me in whispers—doesn't bode well for me.

At the end of the evening, Cathy climbed the stairs to her room. Weary from the day's events, she yawned as she hung her corset on the peg on the wall. She pulled back the blanket on the bed and was about to push her bed companion over for more room when the woman woke up, squealed like a stuck pig, and ran out of the room with eyes wide with fear.

What was that all about? she wondered.

The clip-clop of leather shoes on the wooden floor approached and someone pushed the door open with a bang. Cathy turned around to face the person—there stood the housekeeper, Mrs. Andrews.

"I have no idea what caused her to screech like that," Cathy said.

"She does not want to be in the same room with you," Mrs. Andrews said.

"Why not? I haven't done a thing to her. I don't even know her name."

"She believes you are a bewitcher and is afraid of you," the housekeeper said, as she stood before Cathy with her hands clenched.

"Then she's mistaken. I'm an innocent woman with nothing to hide," Cathy burst out. *Good Lord above, why me? I try to help people and end up getting myself kicked in the butt. When is this going to end?*

"It is late, young lady. Get to bed and this will be discussed in the morning." The housekeeper clip-clopped back to her room.

* * * *

The days dragged by in the dreary kitchen. Cathy's hands were rough and red from harsh soap and constantly being in hot water, and the work days seemed endless.

Bessie had taken to her bed with a toothache. Cathy recommended crushed cloves, taken from the kitchen jar and applied to the aching tooth to relieve the pain.

But Bessie received no relief from the pain, and so the barber had been called in to extract the offending tooth. Cathy had been pressed into duty to fill Bessie's shoes. Being a lower cook was at least a little more interesting than scrubbing pots in a sink of greasy water.

The patient stayed in her bed, with a warm bandage wrapped around her swollen cheek. The tooth extraction had resulted in an abscess in her jaw, which grew steadily worse. Cathy told the housekeeper that she had knowledge of herbs and recommended Bessie be treated with garlic to fight the infection. She had crushed some garlic several times a day, and fed them to Bessie, who swallowed them with the aid of some warm ale. However, following several days of agony, Bessie succumbed to the infection. Her death came as a shock to the other servants in the house.

* * * *

Several days went by with Cathy still being treated as though she were evil, with the servants whispering and snickering in groups around the house. On one afternoon, Cathy had been ordered to draw water from the well located in the center of the courtyard, next to the manor house.

She tied the well's rope to the handle of the wooden bucket and dropped it down the well. She heard a splash and turned the roller handle to bring the pail up to the top of the well. Once at the top, she untied the rope and put the container on the ground. She thought she'd seen a frog sitting on a rock inside the well before dropping into the water, but after running her hands through the water a couple of times, she found nothing and carried the water into the kitchen.

She put the bucket down on the floor as she pivoted the big kettle from over the fire to position it closer to her. Just as she was about to pour the water into the kettle, a small frog jumped out of the water and went splat onto the brick floor. One of the young maids, Nell, leaning over a basin, busily plucking feathers off a chicken, screeched at the sight of the little amphibian and ran behind the large body of the cook.

Cook took one look at the frog and ran over to it with a cleaver in her hand, screaming with each chop of her hand. She chased the small creature and brought down the cleaver a few times, chopping chips out of the brick floor, but she missed the frog every time. "One of you girls take a tea cloth and throw it over the toad. Then throw it into the fire," she screamed.

"It's a little frog from out of the well," Cathy yelled back. "Don't you dare kill it."

"It is a bewitched toad," Cook shrieked. "Kill it!"

"It's an innocent, little, green frog, you cruel, old cow." Cathy fumed.

Jane, the nursemaid, made her appearance at that point. She took stock of the scene before her and sneered, "That toad is her familiar. It must be caught and burned in the fire. She's a witch."

Cathy stopped chasing the women around the kitchen. She stood stock still with shock. "What are you saying? I'm not a witch. I thought you had more brains than to believe in those superstitions."

"Do not speak to me," Jane spat out. "You are an evil, evil, woman in cahoots with the Devil."

"You're out of your mind. I have done nothing to anyone."

"You have bewitched Master Albert into thinking that the captain and others will die on their voyage. He is under your spell and will not listen to others." Jane stood in the middle of the kitchen as she pointed a skinny finger at Cathy.

"That's an outrageous accusation. He's a grown man, able to make his own decisions."

"You also killed Bessie with your magical herbs," Jane screamed. "You are a witch, all right."

"Bessie died of an infection. Nothing could save her," Cathy responded in disbelief.

"You caused her death, and we know not what else you have in store for this household. You have brought your toad, your familiar, with you to assist you in your deadly deeds."

Just then the frog jumped in front of Cathy. She scooped it up and plopped it into her apron's pocket. "I'll put him out in the garden where he'll be safe," Cathy said defiantly, as she walked toward the back door to the garden.

"You see that?" yelled Jane. "It is her familiar. That's why she does not want us to harm it."

"You are all ridiculous," Cathy snapped. She opened the door and placed the little frog in the row of lettuces.

She stepped back into the kitchen, which remained in an uproar. Nell, the young maid, still cowered behind the cook.

"There's nothing to be afraid of," Cathy said to the group. "I'm not a witch or a bewitcher. I'm an ordinary person working hard, just like you."

"That is what all witches say. You have not heard the last of this," Jane barked. She wheeled around and ran up the stairs.

Chapter 5

"Mistress Catherine White?" the well-dressed gentlemen asked as he entered the kitchen.

"Yes, I am she," Cathy answered.

"You should curtsy to the gentleman. He is a constable," Cook whispered to Cathy.

Cathy did a little bob of a curtsy. She gazed at the constable, who wore puffy britches with cuts in them so the yellow underpants showed through, hose, a starched ruff, open at the front, shirt under a doublet, and high-topped boots with square toes. He leaned on his silver-capped walking stick. *Looks like a dandy.*

"Mistress, I have come with disturbing news for you," he began in a solemn tone. He tapped a roll of papers in the open palm of his hand with the silver tip of his cane.

"What is the problem?" Cathy asked.

"Witnesses have sworn to statements accusing you of practicing witchcraft," he stated, as he avoided looking her straight in the eyes.

"Who are these witnesses?" she stammered in disbelief. "No...don't tell me, I can guess who they are—Jane what's-her-name...the nursemaid here at the house, and the kitchen maid, Nell. Right?"

"You are correct."

The cook gasped in disbelief. "Well, I never," she muttered. "Dearie me. Such a bad reputation this house will have. This will bring shame on the household."

"This here in my hand is a warrant for your arrest," the constable continued. He handed her the paper.

Cathy unraveled the rolled paper. The document accused her of bewitching Albert White and Bessie Long with Jane Marsden acting as witness to both acts.

Surely, only a fool would think that she'd bewitched these people. For a moment, she felt confident. *Or, maybe I'm being terribly naïve?* Then fear shuddered through her whole body. She looked up from the paper. She realized these were dangerous times.

"Now please gather your wrap and accompany me," the constable said quietly.

"What? Now?"

"Yes, Mistress White. You are to be imprisoned in the jail at the Market Square straight away."

Cathy pulled her thin shawl off the peg on the wall and draped around her shoulders. "I'm ready," she said softly.

"Follow me."

Cathy followed the constable out into the courtyard where a carriage waited. He helped her up the narrow step and into the small vehicle. She slid across the seat on the black leather, now cracked with age. The constable grunted and panted as he heaved his large body onto the facing seat. The carriage began to move as soon as he had given the signal to the driver.

The wheels rattled and shook the carriage as it made its

way over cobblestone streets. Cathy felt a little "car sick" by the time they reached their destination. Thankfully, it was a short ride, only about a mile, to the jail on the Market Square.

The constable stumbled out of the carriage before her and handed a copy of the warrant to two men who had emerged from the darkened building. The constable stepped back as the men reached into the carriage and pulled Cathy out by her arms. She missed the step and landed on her knees in the wet and dirty street. She struggled to her feet, cursing under her breath.

"Come on, m'dear." One of the men leered in her face. The few teeth that remained in his mouth were green from lack of cleaning.

Disgusting.

"What a pretty little lady we 'ave 'ere," said the second man, putting his hand up her skirt and felt around.

This is going to be hell, she thought, quickly raising her knee and striking him in the crotch. He doubled over and fell on to the ground, moaning in pain.

"Cor, thass un's going to be a 'andful," said the first man while he helped his companion up off the ground.

"We shall see who 'as the last laugh," the second man said, and squeezed Cathy's arm, digging into her flesh with his dirty finger nails, and pulled her into the building.

The jail had been built of stone; stone that stayed cold, no matter the season. Cathy pulled her shawl closer to her body as she tried to warm herself. A small fireplace was located near the front door adjacent to the guard's table, but its heat barely penetrated the chill. Smoky oil lamps burned on three walls. The fourth wall consisted of cells with sliding doors of bars.

The guard she'd kneed shoved her into the first cell—pushing her into the space with a thick truncheon. She stumbled over a woman curled up on the floor, then narrowed her eyes to focus in the dim light and see how many more people were in there. The cell was squalid and smelled like urine.

The guard walked over to a middle-aged woman with an overpowering body odor, who lay slumped over in a corner, too drunk to stand. "Move over there," he screamed at the woman, who stirred and attempted to stand up. The guard struck her over her back with the truncheon. She screamed in pain.

Various other women, of many shapes and sizes, wandered around the cell in circles, shuffling through the straw. The guard pushed Cathy further into the cell, slammed the door shut, and clicked the lock.

"Pickpockets, thieves, and whores," cackled the guard as he leered through the bars. "Nice company to keep, en it, my pretty lass?"

"How long will I have to stay here?" asked Cathy. To say that this imprisonment would not to pleasant would be an understatement, she'd decided.

"You'll be 'ere until your trial, luv. Make yourself comfy."

"I'm hungry," Cathy yelled to the guard. "How do I get some food around here?"

"You 'ave to wait for someone to bring it to ya, or you can pay me, with money or services, and I could go buy ya something to eat."

"But I don't have any money."

"Such a sad story." The guard grinned as he slumped down in his chair and put his feet up on the table. He proceeded to peel an apple with his pocket knife.

She looked around the cell, now that her eyes had become accustomed to the dimness, and spied an empty bench. Making her way over to it, she avoided the other filthy inmates. Her stomach growled in protest as she pulled her knees up into a huddle to make herself look insignificant and thus prevent being abused. She leaned back onto the damp wall and closed her eyes to shut out the disgusting surroundings.

She dozed off for a few minutes.

"Cathy," the voice rang in her ears.

Am I dreaming?

"Cathy. It is Alb. Come over to the door." Alb leaned his face through the bars.

"Watch yourself there," the guard said. "Some of them women will take yer face orf."

Alb stepped back from the bars as he waited for Cathy to come over. He carried a basket in one hand. Cathy's mouth started to water as soon as she saw the basket which, she hoped, held loads of food.

"Alb, I'm so glad to see you."

"I apologize. I was unable to come earlier because I had to serve supper to the family before I could leave."

"Have you told the captain about me?"

"Yes, I have told him the whole story, including your claim you are from the future, and how most of the voyagers will perish in Virginia. He called me a dolt. It was so embarrassing."

"Sometimes it's better to keep your mouth closed. I should never have told you anything." Cathy felt sympathy for him—no, embarrassed by her own actions.

Alb pulled the tea cloth back off the contents of the basket. It held bread, cheese, and a big piece of fruit cake.

"Cook feels sorry for you, so she sneaked this food out. She said she'd try to send food every day for as long as you are locked up here." He gave her a wan smile. "I wish I were rich, then maybe I could pay off the guards and smuggle you out of the country."

"How sweet of you, Alb. Thank Cook for me," Cathy said in between handfuls of food she'd stuffed into her mouth. "Excuse my manners. I have to eat it quickly or those vicious men will take it from me. I had dozed off and jerked awake because they were beating that poor woman over there in the corner and stole her food."

Her fellow inmates eyed the food with envy and drooled as they watched her eat. Cathy had eaten her fill and the basket still contained more food. She carefully broke the bread and cheese into pieces and handed the morsels to the women around her. They muttered brief thanks and then rammed it into their almost toothless mouths. She wrapped the remainder of the cake in her shawl. It would suffice for breakfast because Alb couldn't visit her early tomorrow.

Alb told her he hoped to visit his parents in the morning, but promised he would try to get back to her again later in the day.

If he didn't, she thought she'd rather starve to death than to bargain her services in exchange for food with those disgusting guards.

Chapter 6

Next day, Alb managed to steal away from his work at the manor house because of a lighter work load now that the Gosnold family had left to travel to Otley Hall, the family seat, a few miles away. The captain had explained to his household help about the many noblemen who were on their way to Otley Hall for the meeting to assist him in planning the voyage to Virginia. For Alb, the trial was uppermost in his mind, and this preoccupation had pushed him to decide against volunteering for the expedition with the captain.

The captain's absence from the house enabled Alb to visit his own parents. He doubted he would have another chance for quite some time due to the impending trial of Cathy. His father, a liberal thinker, accepted his son's version of the actions resulting in the accusations, the imprisonment of Cathy, and the imminent court proceedings. Consequently, Alb left his parents' home with reassurance and a pouch full of silver, a gift from his father to be used to make Cathy's situation more endurable.

Alb swore he'd use the money to bribe the guards, and hopefully have Cathy moved to a single cell away from the riff-raff who also occupied the cell. She would require new clothes also.

The other servants in the house had told him that, while he visited his parents, the delegation for the assizes had arrived. The judges, barristers, hangers-on, and servants were met by the town notables near the ruins of the abbey. When the delegation and the nobles met, the men dismounted from their horses, greetings were exchanged, and trumpets were blown.

Later, Cook recalled, the judges, dressed in red robes, left their lodgings and attended church to pray for guidance in the upcoming trials. "I sneaked out and watched them going into the church," Cook added. "Lovely sight it was with all of the judges in scarlet."

Alb advised Cathy of the arrival of the delegation and explained to her that the assizes meant the trial would be held at the court at the Shirehall, near the Great Cemetery.

"The constable came here this morning," Cathy said, scratching the flea bites on her arms. "He said after I had been placed in custody, the court clerk drew up the indictments against me and submitted them to the grand jury. They, in turn, indicted me for bewitching you, and for bringing my familiar, that little frog, into the household, and also for poisoning Bessie with herbs. He entered a not guilty plea for me."

"When are you going to be heard?" Alb asked.

"Tomorrow. At least it'll be over with."

Alb looked forlorn. "Your life may be over with."

She grabbed his hands through the bars. "I'm really scared. I know what most likely will happen to me."

"I, also. My father explained the process to me. It is a capital offense to be blamed of witchcraft. Apparently, it has to do with what is called *maleficium,* using your magic powers to harm your neighbors."

"So I could be found guilty merely because of harmful intent," said Cathy, clearly resigned.

"It is true. The latest statute decreed hanging for maleficent witchcraft. That is just for bewitching a person."

"I don't have a chance." She sighed. "It's so subjective—from the perspective of the witnesses."

Alb shuffled his feet. "My father gifted me some money to help you. I have given some money to the guards so they will move you into a cell at the end of row."

"Thank you, but it hardly seems worth it. I'll only be in it for a day."

"The guards also have been paid to remove you to a back room in the morning. There they will provide you with soap and a bucket of water to enable you to bathe."

"Great. Wouldn't want to smell up the court room," she snapped.

Alb squeezed her hand through the bars. His heart weighed heavy with sadness for her. "Cook has some fresh clothing for you. She is on your side. I will bring it to you tomorrow."

"You've thought of everything," Cathy said. "I will never be able to repay you."

"You are a very special friend to me, Cathy," he said quietly.

* * * *

Cathy bathed and dressed in clean clothes early in the day. The constable arrived in his carriage, which transported her through St. Mary's churchyard to the Shirehall, where the trial was to be held. Crowds gathered in the driveway across from the court and more milled around near the doorway, like vultures waiting for their prey to die.

He pulled her through the entrance hallway by the arm.

"Sit and wait," he commanded as he pushed her to sit on a bench in a small side room. A sign reading Witness Room was affixed to the door on the left of the passageway. The constable took up a position of blocking the door so Cathy wasn't able to escape. She wished she could. Suddenly, the exterior doors flew open and the rabble of spectators rushed through to the two sets of wooden stairs outside the witness rooms. From the clomping of hard leather shoes overhead, she determined the stairs led to the public gallery located above the witness room, where the public could watch the proceedings.

The wait seemed endless for Cathy. Her hands wouldn't stop shaking and nausea swept over her. She could hear the people in the gallery who were jovial for a while, but as more time passed without the trial beginning, they began to stamp their feet.

Then a flurry of flowing robes exited the room on the other side of the hallway. The constable snapped to attention and then turned to Cathy and dragged her from the bench to her feet. "It is time."

"You're hurting me," said Cathy as she shook his huge hand off her arm and glared at him.

"Do what you will, young maiden. Your life will be over soon, so show your defiance now."

He pushed her ahead of him with his cane until they reached the Crown courtroom at the end of the passage. As she entered, a cheer went up from the gallery.

The Shirehall consisted of an L-shaped, two-story timbered building with huge posts supporting the exposed roof timbers. On one wall above the dais on which the judge and sergeant-at-law sat, a large window allowed the daylight to pour into the room. With each movement of the judge's head, powder puffed up from his wig and floated as dust motes in the shafts of sunshine.

The stench from the unwashed public permeated the courtroom, and Cathy suppressed a need to retch. The people in the upstairs public gallery hung over the railings, jeering at her and calling out offensive remarks.

Cathy stood facing the bench. The sergeant-at-law, dressed in violet robes, scratched his scalp beneath his white skull cap; the judge, dressed in crimson, yawned. The jury, all solemn men, trooped in and seated themselves in the jury box at the side of the courtroom.

The court bailiff entered the courtroom and, standing in front of the bench, banged his staff three times on the wooden floor. "Silence. Order in the court," he commanded and waited for the throng to be quiet. Then he positioned himself with legs spread apart in the doorway, blocking all ingress and egress to the courtroom.

Seated in front of the bench, the clerk of arraignment rose and called out, "The court and public request the crier make proclamation."

The crier, standing next to a doorway, looked at the clerk, who nodded for him to begin.

"Here ye all," he yelled. "Silence. All those having business with the court shall draw near and give your attendance. Catherine White shall approach the bar."

Cathy was prodded forward by the bailiff.

"Hold up your right hand," the clerk said and proceeded to read the indictment against her. "The officers of the court and king have sworn that Catherine White did, on the twentieth day of July in the third year of the reign of James the First King of England, bewitch one Albert White and feloniously cause, by bewitchment, the death of one Bessie Long." His voice droned on and on, while the heat and stench made Cathy feel faint.

"How do you plead?" demanded the clerk.

She jerked to attention.

"Guilty or not guilty?"

"Not guilty," she said with defiance, straightening her back and squaring her shoulders.

"God send thee a good deliverance." The bailiff shoved her backwards into the prisoner's box.

The crier stepped forward and called out, "All those who have information of the charges come forth and they shall be heard, for now the prisoner stands upon her deliverance."

"The prosecutor calls the Crown witness Jane Marsden, nurse maiden to the children of Captain Bartholomew Gosnold, to the dock to give evidence of the accused's bewitching," said the clerk.

An elderly man was perched on a high stool at an equally high desk as he wrote notes of the trial. At quiet times in the courtroom, the scrivener's quill could be heard scratching on the parchment.

Jane, with head set at an arrogant nose-in-the-air angle, walked up the steps into the dock which was a high, box-like structure. Her appearance would be comical under any condition other than this trial. She wore a gaudy, red lacey dress and had powdered her face white with red circles of rouge on her cheeks. Her teeth were yellow against the ghostly makeup.

As the clerk swore in the witness, Cathy groaned inwardly. *This grotesque, clown-like woman holds my future in her hands.*

The prosecutor faced the dock, where the witness was forced to stand. "Tell the court what you know of the be-witching by the prisoner of persons at the place of your employment."

Jane straightened her back and in a clear voice said, "This woman, Catherine White, has bewitched the footman in our household. His name is Albert White, but, I am sorry to say, he is still so bewitched that he cannot attend this trial. The prisoner told him that she is from the future, which he be-lieves. He does not believe her to be a fortuneteller or a witch, despite our arguments."

A gasp went up in the gallery, where the crowd had grown quiet, straining their ears to catch each word from the dock.

"Let the court note that the footman has failed to appear forthwith," the prosecutor stated. "Please continue," he urged Jane in a fatherly tone.

Jane nodded.

"And it was a few weeks ago that she brought her familiar into the kitchen—a huge, ugly toad—her imp. Cook and the others tried to catch it or hit it with a broom, but were unable to. We wanted to pitch it into the fire but that woman—" She pointed to Cathy. "—screeched, saying that it was merely a little frog and she protected it from being thrown into the fire. She caught the creature in a cloth and hid it outside in the garden, out of harm's way."

"That's a lie!" Cathy screamed. "It was merely a little frog."

"Silence," yelled the judge.

"But she is lying. When will I have someone to defend me?"

"There shall be no examination of the witness. Defendants are not permitted to have lawyers," the judge snapped.

Wonderful, Cathy thought. *I'm not allowed a lawyer and so can't cross-examine the witness to defend myself. There's no hope for me.*

Jane had a smug look on her face as she continued, "Bessie Long is—was—the under cook at the manor house. One day she complained of a toothache."

"And then what did the prisoner do?"

"She put crushed cloves on the tooth."

"Did that cure the under cook?"

"No, it made the tooth ache more. We requested the barber to come and pull it out."

"Then what happened?"

"The offending tooth was removed, but Bessie's cheek swelled. Catherine White tendered garlic to the girl. It did not help and Bessie screamed in pain and spat out crooked pins—put there by that witch. Then she died." With trembling fingers, she pointed at Cathy.

"That's not true. She had an infection that killed her. I was trying to heal her," Cathy screamed.

"Silence." The bailiff slapped his thin cane on the prisoner's box, making Cathy jump. "The judge has spoken and you will be silent."

"These are the facts set before you, Your Honor," the prosecutor said as he faced the judge. "We have no more witnesses."

Cathy was dumbfounded. *Only one witness who told ridiculous lies?*

The judge cleared his throat and turned to face the jury.

"I will not sway your opinions by repeating the evidence which, I believe, is clear. Witches are everywhere, not only in this place, but also in other countries, where they have been put to death. I am of the opinion that the prisoner employed evil means to feloniously bewitch, enchant and poison the unfortunate Bessie Long, living within the peace of God in the household of the Honorable Bartholomew Gosnold. She has utilized her familiar imp, in the disguise of a toad, for diabolical purposes to bewitch the footman, who is bewitched and languishes still."

The judge sneezed and blew his nose noisily in a grubby handkerchief, which he then stuffed into his sleeve for safe-keeping. He continued, "But it is, however, your burden to determine the guilt or innocence of the accused woman as a common witch and enchantress."

The judge appears to be intelligent, but he accepted all those fabricated facts as the truth? God help me. She choked back tears.

The trial had only taken a couple of hours. The jury reached their decision quickly and relayed their verdict of guilty of bewitchment.

The court clerk read the passing of the sentence. Cathy was stunned. She couldn't believe she'd had been found guilty on the flimsy testimony of one woman. The evidence was laughable in light of the beliefs in the present day—but she wasn't in the present. She was caught in a nightmare once more.

Help me! She would die before she could return to Al. She broke down into tears.

The clerk's voice droned on and on in Cathy's head as he read the sentence, "...and pled not guilty. Upon evidence given, said accused was found guilty and thereupon received judgment to die for same. *Suspendendae per collum*—to be hanged by the neck."

Cathy fainted.

* * * *

The hanging was to be held in the town square. Whole families had traveled into town from the country villages to see the execution, which was considered good entertainment.

Street vendors hawked meat pies, fruit pies, and pig bladders, blown up to resemble balloons, tied to sticks. Groups of young boys kicked around animal bladders like soccer balls. Other peddlers sold rotten fruit and vegetables to be thrown at the prisoner.

The guards allowed Cathy to sit near the doorway of the jail, catching her last rays of sunshine.

"Time to go," jeered one of the jailers.

Alb helped her stand. He then took her face in his hands and gently kissed her on her lips. Tears streamed down her cheeks.

"I shall remember you always," he whispered. "We will meet again."

"Thank you for everything, Alb," she sobbed. "It wouldn't have been bearable without you."

He helped her climb up into the solid-wheeled wagon. A large shire horse was harnessed up and ready to pull the cart through the crowd. Cathy grabbed hold of the front of the wagon, which jerked as the horse started forward.

The crowd had waited several hours for the entertainment to begin and they'd grown impatient and quite unruly. Several constables and sheriffs had been gathered from the rest of the county to assist in keeping the crowd under control. It was soon obvious the officials were outnumbered by several hundreds of people. A witch's hanging was a favorite.

The horse could only take a few steps at a time, for fear people in the crowd would be trampled if the cart moved any faster. Bang. A cabbage hit Cathy's head, followed by a rotten tomato that smashed and ran down over her face. She turned around to see Alb struggling through the crowd toward the cart.

"Alb!" she shrieked.

"I will help you," he yelled to her.

"Witch," someone shouted from the crowd.

"Hang her."

"Burn her."

"Hanging's too good for a witch."

Eggs smashed into her shoulder. Rotten fruit smacked her back and dripped down her clothes.

Alb managed to break through the crowd and clambered onto the tumbrel. The crowd pushed up against the cart and began to rock it back and forth. He held onto the sides as he made his way over to Cathy and took her in his arms. She shook uncontrollably.

"Evil woman," an old man screeched.

"Get your familiar to save you now," a voice taunted her from the crowd.

Several men carried large wooden clubs studded with nails. They approached the wagon screaming insults and curses at her. One grabbed the reins of the horse only to be whipped by the driver with the long whip he carried. "Get back," he ordered, lashing out at the men.

It was no use. The men unhitched the horse from the cart and led it by the reins to the other side of the square. The driver turned to his passengers. "Lie down," he bellowed. "They're coming back. They're carrying cudgels."

Alb gripped Cathy's shoulders and pushed her onto the floor of the wagon. "Stay down," he yelled in her ear. The noise of the crowd was deafening as it roared around them.

"I'm afraid, Alb," she cried. "Please hold me close."

"I am with you, my darling."

It began to rock again. Cathy and Alb rolled from side-to-side as they tried to brace themselves against the sides of the tumbrel. The howling continued. Vegetables and fruit rained on the couple locked together in each others arms. Crash! A large rock smacked the wooden sides.

"They're throwing stones and rocks now," Cathy wailed over the din. "Oh, no. More of them have clubs! They're going to kill—" Her sentence was cut short as a crushing blow hit her head. The man raised his club again to strike again. Alb grabbed the man and kicked him away from the cart.

Too late, she thought through a haze. Her scalp spurted blood. She tried to cry out to Alb, but nothing came out of her mouth. *It's happening again. Is this the end of my life?*

The sounds of a flute floated through the daze. *Al, Ed, Alb.*

Crunch. A rock smashed her head. She could hear a woman cackling, "Witch. Die, die, die." The noise of the tumultuous crowd began to recede back into her head until it became a mere echo. Then she heard nothing.

The Dragonfly

Part IV

The Dragonfly

Chapter 1

June, 1943

"Come on, girl!" Sheila gently slapped the woman's face. She was flat on her back where she'd fallen. "Wake up. Don't scare me like this."

Cathy's eyelids fluttered.

"That's right. Wake up. Come on, girl." Sheila pulled a handkerchief out of the pocket of her khaki breeches. She reached over to the water jug and sloshed some of the liquid onto the hankie. She dabbed Cathy's face with the wet cloth to clean off the dirt, and, hopefully, to shock the woman back to consciousness.

Sheila and an elderly farm worker had gathered the hay, which had been cut and dried in the field, using the horse-drawn hay rake. They had discovered Cathy wandering down the country lane that lead to the farm's wheat fields. Sheila tried not to ridicule the woman dressed in a long, muddy skirt and a bodice above which her breasts mounded.

Looks like she's from a gypsy camp. Must've been in a beauty of an argument. The woman had dried blood on her face and caked in her hair and had no clue as to where she was. Sheila and her helper loaded her onto the cart on top of a pile of hay, destined to be built into a haystack. One huge, plodding Suffolk Punch draft horse pulled the cart. Sheila led the chestnut-colored horse by its reins while the wagon bumped with every rut the wheels hit.

Cathy yelled, "Huge dip coming up!" when she was suddenly dumped onto the ground by the lurching contraption.

Cathy moaned. "Where am I?" She pulled herself up, leaned back on her elbows, and stared at Sheila.

"You're in Lackford. For a minute there, I thought you were dead."

"Lackford? My mother lived here when she was a little girl. How did I get here? I don't understand. I'm so confused." Cathy shook her head. Sheila grabbed her by the hand and pulled her to her feet. Cathy attempted to brush dirt off her skirt, but it was no use.

"The last thing I remember is being in a cart on my way to a funeral. I think that's where I was going."

"Boy, that crack on your head really addled your brain. There's no funeral here." Sheila stared at her and her co-worker shrugged his shoulders. "You don't look too steady on your pins. You should have a doctor look at you. I'll have to talk about that with Mr. Wilson."

"I'm fine. Just have a splitting headache. Ouch! Maybe a sprained ankle." Cathy limped over the ruts in the field and leaned on the side of the cart. "I'm just puzzled is all. You're sure there's no funeral in the village today?" She didn't want to confess to this person that she was on her way to her *own* funeral.

"Absolutely sure. We just came through the meadow next to the church. There's no one there. Honest."

Cathy looked at Sheila's clothes. "Is this some kind of uniform?"

"I'm in the Women's Land Army." Sheila laughed. "Really attractive, aren't I?"

"Bloody awful, if you ask me. What's a Land Army?"

"You're pulling my leg, I know, but I'll go along with your joke." Sheila grinned. "The Land Army's a bunch of women who joined up because we were told it was glamorous to work the land by manning the farms and get paid a peasant's pittance to help the war effort. All able-bodied farmhands are off fighting. So here we are!"

Cathy stared at the other woman in disbelief. "Really? What war is this?"

"World War II, you big dollop! It's 1943. Surely you know what year it is?" Sheila looked worried as she held onto Cathy's arm to give her some stability on the uneven ground. "Come on. Lean on me and I'll lead the horse and cart. Have to get it back to the stables and then figure out what we're going to do with you."

"1943," Cathy mumbled. "Getting closer to home."

"What was that?"

"Oh, nothing important."

The couple slowly made their way back to the farm's main buildings by way of the grassy lane that bordered the field. Sheila led the huge horse, while Cathy hobbled as she held onto her other arm.

Mr. Wilson, the farm's foreman, met them in the stables' forecourt. Sheila relayed the news about finding this woman and her fall off the cart and, in turn, he stared at Cathy's dirty and bruised face. When he heard that Cathy thought she'd been on the way to the funeral, with a click of his tongue, he uttered a local expression, "Thass a rummun," meaning that's strange.

He strode to the other side of the cobblestone forecourt and pushed a motorcycle over to where the women were standing.

"Better get in the sidecar, young lady, and I'll run you over to Alice Frost's—she's me sister," he said in a thick Suffolk accent which made sidecar sound like "soidcar" and I'll became "oil." "She's lookin' for a lodger and she'll nurse yer bad head."

Cathy protested. She didn't want to climb into the tiny sidecar balanced on one wheel. It looked dangerous—like a bomb attached to one side of the ancient motorcycle. Sheila, who lived about half a mile down the road, insisted that Cathy let Wilson drive her to Alice's home.

"We can't just leave you on the side of the road. You need somewhere to stay until you remember who you are. That's a nasty bump coming up on your head," Sheila added. "I'll ride over on my bicycle later to see how you are. I'm supposed to go to a dance tonight. Wanna go? If you're feeling better that is."

"Where's the dance?"

"In the village hall—we can go by bicycle. Alice probably has one you can borrow."

"Sounds like it would be fun," Cathy said with a shrug of her shoulders as she squeezed herself into the narrow seat of the sidecar. She put on the goggles handed to her by Wilson and clung on for dear life as the motorcycle roared to life. It took less than five minutes to arrive at the cottage on the other side of the village. She clambered out by swinging first one leg and then the other over the side of the sidecar. She was glad she wore a long skirt; otherwise her disembarking would have created a very unladylike sight.

Wilson slouched down the pathway leading to the cottage's front door. There, he held a short conversation with the woman who opened the door, apparently his sister, who nodded and smiled in Cathy's direction.

Wilson walked back to his motorcycle and gave a pedal a crank with his foot. "Alice said she'll take you in," he yelled over the loud engine noise.

"Thanks," she called out to Wilson as he disappeared up the road in a dust cloud. *Now to meet Mrs. Frost,* Cathy thought as she walked gingerly down the path to the low front door of the cottage. She could feel the bruises coming out on her hip and ankle.

"Cathy? My brother said you've been in an accident. Come on in. I've been looking for a lodger, and it looks like you were just dropped down from heaven onto my doorstep," said the woman. "Think of this as your home."

"Mrs. Frost?"

The woman held the door open wide. "Yes, but you may call me Alice."

Cathy stepped down onto the brick floor, crossed the small room, and sat down on a wooden chair. She explained to Alice how she'd fallen off the cart and hit her head.

Cathy hoped her head injuries would camouflage her so-called lack of memory. She wasn't ready to tell people that she came from another time.

"What you need is a good cup of tea. Have a nice lie down on the sofa and rest while I make it," Alice said. "Do you have your ration book, dear?"

"Sorry, I have nothing but the clothes on my back."

"And strange they are—must have been to a fancy dress party."

"I don't remember," Cathy lied.

"Well, never mind, love. Tomorrow we'll go to the borough hall and get a temporary ration book for you."

"Good idea." Cathy yawned and moved over onto the sofa, plumped up a pillow under her head, and stretched out her aching body. She fell fast asleep in a few minutes.

* * * *

Alice looked over at the exhausted girl and shook her head. She filled the tea kettle from the pail of water in the pantry. Then she struggled with two big metal pails of water, putting them to heat on the coal stove.

Alice Frost, born and bred in the village, was a typical woman trying to survive hard times minus a husband. Her husband, a sergeant in the British Army, was serving his time somewhere on one of the many battlefronts in Europe. His few letters home would mention the general location of his regiment, but the censors, who read every piece of mail leaving the fronts, would black out most of the letters. So, like all other families, they really never did know the whereabouts of their loved ones. All she knew was that life was hard back in England.

Alice shoved the poker into the bottom of the stove grate and rattled out the coal ashes. She took the lid lifter, inserted it into the hole in the lid and opened the top of the old, black cast-iron stove, and dumped in a few lumps of coal. She moved the big tea kettle over to the hot top to boil.

It would be nice, she'd told a neighbor, to have a lady lodger stay with her. The best part was she could use the woman's coupon book. The coupons, good for four weeks, would be a great help to Alice and her little girl, Rose. It would not only stretch the rations on sugar, bacon, tea, and butter, it would also allow her to buy more coal to keep at bay the rising damp of the draughty, although picturesque, thatched cottage. Just those few extra lumps of coal at night in the stove would make all the difference to the temperature in the sitting room.

It was a stretch to call the room a sitting room because it also served as the kitchen, dining room, and a place where they took their baths. All their food was cooked on the big cast-iron stove, which also was the only source of heat. In order to have cooked food and hot tea, the stove had to stay alight even through the summer. Summers tended to be cool, though, so it didn't cause a problem.

The kettle came to a boil quickly. Alice poured the hot water over the pile of tea leaves in the large, brown teapot. She covered the teapot with a knitted tea cozy (re-knitted from an old pullover she'd taken apart for the yarn) and set out the cups and saucers on the table. She stepped over to the sofa.

"Wake up. Time for tea." She shook the sleeping young woman.

* * * *

Cathy stretched her long arms and legs. "Ow! I should've stayed awake. My whole body is stiff now."

"C'mon, dear." Alice pulled out a wooden chair. "Sit here at the table and have your tea."

Cathy took a few faltering steps over to the proffered chair and gingerly sat on the hard seat. "Thanks. I need this."

Alice held on to the lid and poured out the hot tea into the cups.

"You'll feel right as rain soon." She acted motherly, although she was only a few years older than Cathy. "You do have some nasty bruises coming out on your forehead, though."

Cathy put her hand up to her face to feel the swelling. "I hope I don't look like a freak. Sheila wants me to go to the dance at the village hall tonight."

"Do you think that's wise?"

"I'm fine. Once I've bathed, I'll feel like a normal person." Cathy laughed.

"I've got the bath water on already, dear." Alice pointed with her head to the pails on the stove.

"The 'dears' laid some eggs this morning, so we have a lovely tea today," she continued, referring to the aging chickens she kept.

The older the hens got, she told Cathy, the smaller the eggs became, but were appreciated as much-needed sustenance in these times of food shortages. "If you don't have laying hens, you're rationed to one or two a week, or worse, dried eggs," she added with a grimace. "But 'cause I've got less than twenty chickens, I'm allowed to keep all the eggs they lay. I save the extras we don't use right away in a pail of water glass preserve in the pantry. Good for cooking."

Cathy nodded as she sipped the hot, sweet tea. She smiled as she looked at the center of the table. Three small brown eggs were lined up, sitting in matching white eggcups, wearing brightly colored knitted cozies to keep them warm. They looked like children wearing wool hats.

Little Rose kicked her wooden high chair and held out both of her arms. "Me, me."

"Here, darling," Alice said. She took the cozy off one of

the eggs, cracked the shell with a spoon, removed the top, and dipped into the soft-boiled egg with a sliver of toast. She popped it into the child's mouth.

"At least we have eggs from the chickens and vegetables from the garden. Today, Mr. Hurrell from next door brought me a rabbit he'd trapped. That'll make a good dinner for us tomorrow. Lucky we live in the country, I s'pose." She pushed a lock of hair that had escaped from the kerchief tied around her head off her face. "Don't know how those poor people in cities are faring. Lord Woolton keeps saying on the radio to only eat what you need, then you'll be helping to win the war. S'all right for him…he probably has plenty to eat."

"It must be difficult with the food shortage."

"Good gracious me!" Alice burst out. "Of course it's difficult. This darned war's been going on for years now."

Cathy jumped, surprised by the woman's reaction. *She must be more careful how she asked questions,* she told herself. She couldn't depend on the head injury excuse covering up her ignorance forever.

"Shortages are making things hard! Rationing's on everything. You obviously didn't do the shopping at home, young lady."

"No, you're right. Mum did everything for me," Cathy fibbed. "She coddled me. Kept me from reality, I suppose."

"Even the poor pets are suffering," Alice continued. "I read in the papers that thousands of dogs were put to sleep in the first fortnight of the war. No food for them. Cats can always catch mice."

"Good gracious. How awful!" Cathy said with a catch in her throat. She hadn't thought of how food shortages and war could affect pets and other animals.

"'Course people like the squire have sent their dogs to Donegal in Ireland to wait for the end of the war. Nice to have money." She sniffed.

The two women sat silent for a moment.

"When will this war be over?" Cathy posed the hypothetical question with a sigh.

She was about to put a mouthful of toast in her mouth when a loud knock startled her.

Bang, bang, bang.

A heavy hand thudded on the door. Alice jumped up from the table, hurried over to the casement window and pulled back the white lace curtains.

"It's the battery man—for the wireless," she announced. "He's late today."

"Battery man?"

"Yes, grab the battery in the pantry for me, will you? I'll get the door."

Cathy went into the narrow room she assumed was the pantry. Along the walls were shelves lined with newspaper pages with edges jauntily cut into points. No one had any luxuries, she observed, but they made do and prettied-up however they could. She spotted a square glass object on the floor which resembled a small car battery with a handle. *Batteries will come as small as your little finger fifty years from now,* she thought. She lugged the battery over to the door and handed it to the waiting man.

"Thanks. Now I can listen to ITMA and the news again," Alice said.

The battery man handed a recharged battery into Alice's awaiting arms. He wore tan coveralls that were full of holes, probably burnt through by battery acid. He pulled out a small book and pencil from his breast pocket, licked his pencil, checked off the delivery, and tucked the pencil behind his ear. "See you next week," he said and stalked off down the path.

"What's an ITMA?" Cathy asked as she closed the door.

"It's not a what, dear. *It's That Man Again* is a funny program on the wireless."

Alice opened the back on the radio set, hooked up the battery, turned it on, and waited for the tubes to warm up. The wooden radio came alive with a whistle and a crack as she turned the knob to tune it into a station.

"I love Tommy Handley. I laugh 'til tears run down my cheeks. Your family too posh to listen to that program?"

"No, they're not elitist at all." Cathy quickly conjured up a family in her head. She thought of her own mother, Janice, a small, delicate, blonde widow, who must be worried sick about her missing daughter. Janice had always been fragile and would shudder to know that her daughter now lived in the war years. She had hideous memories of the war and she'd never forgiven the whole country of Germany for not standing up against the evil Hitler, for obeying that madman's orders, in fact, for stealing her childhood. "I suppose Mum never listened to it, that's all."

"Shame," Alice said and sniffed. "S'funny." She brushed food crumbs off the tablecloth into her other hand. "You've heard people say TTFN—ta-ta for now, haven't you? They started TTFN on that program."

"Of course I've heard it," Cathy answered defensively. In fact, her mother never used the term ta-ta for goodbye, but she had to keep up her façade. "We say TTFN all the time."

Time to change the subject, Cathy thought. She made a mental note not to ask so many questions. *Look and listen first,* she vowed. If she wasn't careful, everyone would tag her as either a mental case or an eccentric. All she wanted was to get back to her husband. *Al, Al, please help me come back to you,* she prayed. She yearned to have his strong arms around her, with his soft kisses on her lips. Safe in his embrace.

She daydreamed as she finished eating. In the research done for her paper, she'd read so much about health problems the people endured during WWII. She had to act as though she wasn't cognizant of those facts from her retrospective view of history. The clattering of plates jarred her back to reality.

"Let me help you clear the table, and I'll do the dishes," Cathy said as she helped pile the plates onto each other.

"No need. The bath water is already boiling, dear."

"Then what can I do to help?"

"You can help me bring in the bath. It's heavy for one person. I usually drag it in myself, but the bottom's getting ruined from scraping on the ground."

The two women went outside, walked past the well near the front door, and the outside toilet to the side of the cottage. Swallows' mud nests clung to the eaves overhanging the thatched roof. The galvanized steel bathtub hung by its handle on a big nail on the side of the house. Next to it hung a smaller version, for children, she supposed. They carefully took the large bath off the nail, making sure not to bang it on their shins. Alice held onto the front handle in the front and led the way with Cathy holding onto the other handle. After stumbling down the doorstep, they deposited the bath in front of the stove.

Alice set up a fabric-covered screen around one side of the bath, which added some privacy and kept the fire's warmth close to the bather. She then crushed some egg shells into tiny pieces which she used to scrub out the tub. The water in the pails bubbled on the stove.

"Water's ready and the cobwebs have been cleaned out," Alice announced as she grabbed a couple of potholders. She poured the boiling water into the tub, being careful not to splash any on the floor. "Bring out the pail of cold water from the pantry, would you, dear?" Cathy brought the bucket and gradually poured some of it into the bath as she tested for the appropriate temperature. "Here's an old dressing gown you can use."

Little Rose sucked on her thumb as she watched her mother prepare the bath. "Lovely and warm," said Alice as she peeled the clothes off the toddler. "In you pop, love." She scattered Lux detergent flakes onto the little girl's head and gently massaged it into her hair. "Can't wait for real shampoo, when this war's over." Then, Little Rose got soaped up quickly, rinsed and picked up, wet and slick, in her mother's arms and swaddled in a towel.

The air in the room had cooled, so Cathy undressed behind the screen as quickly as she could in the warmth of the fire and eased herself into the metal tub. The warm water felt good on her aches and pains. Reluctantly, she shampooed her hair with the detergent. It was still better than what she'd had to use in the past, though. She wished she could just soak in the warm water for about an hour, but it wasn't possible, so she washed, and sloshed herself with the sponge to rinse off as best she could in the soapy water. Alice still had to have her bath using the same water.

Cathy stepped out of the water and wrapped herself in a towel and peeked around the screen.

"Your turn," she said.

"Thanks for not lingering!" Alice said as she took her turn in the bath.

"Don't you wish you could have a bath all to yourself?" Cathy asked.

"Of course I would," Alice answered from the other side of the screen, "but it's not possible nowadays. Not enough coal to heat that much water. At least we have our own well—no rations on that. My sister in London is only allowed to put five inches of water into her bath. Rule when you live in a town, you know. She's painted a black line at five inches so the kids won't overfill the bath."

"That's barely enough to wash yourself in." Cathy briskly rubbed her hair with the towel. She wished she had an electric hair dryer, but since this cottage didn't even have electricity, she had to be satisfied with drying her curls the old-fashioned way.

"Like I said, we're lucky to have a lovely deep bath. Mustn't moan about it," Alice said as she splashed water over herself. "Would like to soak my feet a little longer. My corns are killing me from my shoes. They were really my sister's— the shoes, not the corns. I needed shoes, so she gave me this pair. My everyday pair of shoes has holes in the soles, so I put cardboard in them and I can still wear them. Can't wear them when it's raining 'cause the cardboard gets wet." There was more splashing as she rose out of the water. "We were told to varnish the soles of our shoes to make them last longer, but all it did was make them slippery! Can't complain, though."

Cathy made concurring noises.

"Put your dressing gown on, would you, dear?" Alice walked around the screen as she wrapped herself in her warm robe. "I need help dumping the water into the garden."

"Of course." Cathy quickly tied the cord on her robe.

Cathy grabbed hold of one handle, and with Alice hanging onto the other one, they sloshed their way out into the flower garden, grunting with exertion.

Just as they were tipping out the soapy water, a loud roar sounded overhead. Cathy looked up, astonished. Only a few feet above them flew a small propeller plane with a painted swastika on its tail. The pilot, his head swathed in a leather helmet and big dark goggles, cheerily waved to them.

"Bloody Gerry," screamed Alice, shaking her fist at the plane. "Probably dropping tinfoil to knock out the radar—the kids'll be busy now picking it up and taking it to school for collection. The planes come in so low hedgehopping through the fields, it's a wonder they don't hit the cows."

Cathy just stood there with her mouth open, as she marveled at the amazing sight.

Chapter 2

Alice showed her up to the bedroom she was to use. It was a space on the large upstairs landing of the cottage and had been Alice's younger sister's room prior to her joining the army.

"Jane was an army nurse stationed at Coventry. She was killed two years ago, when the German Luftwaffe bombed the city."

"Oh, how sad," Cathy said with a sigh.

"Yes, I miss her every day." Alice wiped away a stray tear. "Now, let's get you settled. When they called you up, did you choose armed forces, farming or factories?"

"I don't remember," Cathy lied. "But I probably chose farming. That's where my interest lies."

"We'll take care of that tomorrow when we go into town." Alice banged the bed pillows, fluffing them. "You're welcome to anything of Jane's in the wardrobe. Her clothes are too small for me. I've got a bigger bum," she said, patting her hips as she descended the stairs.

"Thanks." Cathy looked around.

The bedroom was set into the thatched roof, the walls slanted up to the peak. A tiny window was about ten feet up from the floor, not affording any good chance of proper lighting, but enough for daytime activities. To provide some privacy, Alice had hung a curtain on a line of string strung from one side of the space to the other. A bed stood in the middle of the floor dressed in a fluffy, feather mattress covered with a satin eiderdown.

A pure white chamber pot with a sturdy handle peeked out from under the bed. *Yuck. I'll hold everything or feel my way in the dark to the outside lavatory rather than use the guzunder, as locals call it.*

Daylight was fading quickly. In order to delay the lighting of the paraffin lamp on the dresser, Cathy decided to put on her makeup before she dressed. She found a pot of face cream and beige powder in the dresser's top drawer, together with a tube of bright red lipstick. Although not really her color, she decided it was better than nothing. She smeared the cream all over her face. It felt soothing on her bruises. She patted some face powder on her shiny nose and bruised forehead. Then she pouted her lips and added some lipstick to her lips. It resembled a red slash on her powder-whitened face. She shrugged her shoulders at her ghoulish image in the mirror.

Cathy opened the second drawer of the dresser and pulled out a full slip. It slid easily down her body. It fit perfectly. Then she took a plain blue dress out of the armoire. This, too, fit her like a glove. She posed in front of the full-length mirror on the wall. It was a short, pretty dress, swooped up in the front to one side, a sweetheart neckline, and padded shoulders.

"Shades of Joan Crawford," she said out loud as she smiled at her image.

The deceased Jane's wardrobe was packed with clothes

for all seasons and reeked of camphor moth balls. The smell reminded her of her grandmother.

She ran a comb through her hair. The dark curls bounced back in place, now dry and shiny. Glancing at the hairstyle on the model on the front page of a magazine lying on the dresser, she swept the sides of her hair back with combs. Looking in the mirror, she turned her head from side to side. *Looks really forties. I'll pass for the genuine thing.*

"Coo-ee!" The shrill voice of Alice rang up the stairs. "Sheila's here, and she brought along a bicycle for you."

"Thanks, Alice! I'll be right down," Cathy called back down.

She dabbed some lavender *eau de cologne* onto the corner of an embroidered hanky, discovered a black purse on the shelf in the wardrobe and tucked it under her left arm as she slipped into the sensible, thick-heeled, navy blue shoes she found under the bed. Her ankle was barely swollen now, and the pain had subsided. Careful to place her unfamiliar shoes squarely on the narrow, rickety bare-wood steps leading downstairs, Cathy slowly made her way down to the living room.

Sheila stood in the doorway. The light shone through the filmy silk dress she wore.

"You'll pick up a lot of boyfriends looking like that," Cathy said while smiling at her new friend.

"What do you mean?" Shelia asked as she stepped down, wobbling in her high heels on the brick floor.

"You can see right through your dress!"

"Really? That's all right with me." Sheila giggled. "I'll have more interested Brylcreem boys than you then."

Cathy gave her a quizzical look.

"You'll have more men buzzing around you," Sheila explained, "because you're prettier than I am. So this'll even out the playing field."

"Come on." Cathy felt her face heat with a blush. "With your green eyes and lovely long, red hair, who could resist you?"

"Tons of freckles come with the flaming hair." Sheila wrinkled her nose while she plumped her hair in the mirror hanging over an old dresser.

"Oh, dear, Cathy, look at your legs," piped up Alice.

"What's wrong with them? My bruises aren't showing, are they?"

"No, but you aren't wearing stockings."

"So?"

"I'm not wearing stockings either," interjected Sheila. "We'll put leg makeup on next time we go out."

"Yes...no time today." Cathy turned to Sheila. "How did you get two bikes here?"

"I rode mine, holding onto the handlebar with my left hand and pushed yours with my right hand. S'easy!" Sheila said with a grin. "It was just sitting in the barn, so I borrowed it."

"Thanks. I won't have to walk to the dance."

"We could always go in Wilson's soidcar, though!" Sheila said imitating the old man's accent. "Ready to go?"

"Yep, all ready for my big night on the town." Cathy smiled.

"It beats shoveling cow manure."

They wheeled their bicycles down the path. Hollyhocks nodded their blooms like bonnets, while black-faced purple and pink pansies stared at them from the flower border. The garden gate clicked shut behind them.

"Stay on the side of the road," shouted Alice at the couple as they slowly pedaled away down the road, "and make sure you don't come home too late. Your bikes have no lights. Cars won't be able to see you."

"Will do!" they shouted back, and with a wave they rounded the corner, and the concerned Alice was hidden from view.

They blithely spun along the country road, laughing at each other's remarks, while their hair blew around their faces in the breeze. The fields on both sides of the road looked like a patchwork quilt—bright yellow mustard plants in bloom, then golden with ripe wheat, then green polka-dotted with red poppies, each patch separated by straight-trimmed hedgerows. A black-and-white magpie flew down to the grassy verge and pecked at a hapless insect.

Cathy hadn't felt this relaxed and carefree for so long. It felt like she'd been on this journey back through time for years. She wondered how long she'd been gone, and when she'd ever get back to Al. She wished she knew the answers, but, for now, she'd enjoy this fun evening with her friend.

They rode through the village by the Holden's manor house, the Norman village church, St. Lawrence, and rows of thatched cottages. *Those charming cottages will be worth a fortune in sixty years,* Cathy mused, *but right now they're uncomfortable, unheated, drafty relics with leaky roofs.*

A lorry put-putted by them, the back loaded with cages of chickens. Chickens—screeching, squawking, with eyes wide with terror, their feathers flying out onto the road, on the way to their deaths at the slaughterhouse. Cathy shuddered and felt nauseated. Her subconscious kept rambling, like a stream.

"Cathy…Cathy!" Sheila yelled at her.

Cathy jerked herself back to reality, braked her bicycle and dismounted. Shaken, she was back to the present.

"Watch out!" yelled Sheila. "There's a car coming up behind us."

Cathy quickly moved closer to the side of the road as an old car, from the 1930s, packed full with British servicemen, chugged by them, swerving to avoid hitting the two on bicycles. All the car's windows were open. One of the young men hung halfway out a back window.

"Sorry," he yelled with an impish grin and a wave of a uniformed arm.

"Bloody idiots," Sheila back screamed at him.

"That was close," Cathy gasped as Sheila pulled up beside her.

"They could've killed us," Sheila said dramatically. "I hope they're going to the dance, so I can really give them a piece of my mind."

"Whoa, girl. Don't overreact. Nothing happened, so relax."

"I guess you're right. Crazy drivers just make me nuts."

"Why don't we just push our bikes and walk the rest of the way to the village hall?"

"Good idea," Sheila puffed. "It gives me a chance to cool down my temper."

They soon arrived, and shoved their bikes up the thick-with-gravel driveway. On the back wall of the building there were about a dozen other bicycles, all interwoven into what resembled a metal, modern sculpture.

"Gawd help you if you have to leave early," Sheila said with a laugh. "It'll take you forever to get your own bike out of this mess."

For that reason they decided to lean them together against the concrete cones set up on the corner of the grass to keep moving tanks from plowing into the structure.

The women walked around the building and entered via the porch entrance, a place to shuck your wet boots and stow umbrellas in inclement weather, and pushed through the crowd clustered around the door.

Strains of big-band music blared out of the speaker of an old gramophone. Cathy recognized a Duke Ellington rendition of an old song. She smiled as she thought about the stereo boom boxes and portable CD players to come in the future. It felt like reminiscing, but could you reminisce about the future?

Despite being in a room crowded with people, loneliness crept into her whole being. *So homesick.* She wanted to go home to her family and friends. Her heart ached for Al. Tears flooded her eyes as she took in the scene, so she turned her face away from Sheila, who would not understand why she cried.

Young girls, gathered into a swirling wave of moving pastel summer frocks, giggled and gawked at the crowd of servicemen lined up on the opposite wall. The young men were of assorted ages from pimply eighteen-year-olds to more sophisticated men in their late twenties with David Niven mustaches. Most of them were in dark blue, Royal Air Force uniforms and sported hair plastered down on their heads with gobs of hair cream.

"Ooh, we have a nice lot of Brylcreem boys this week," yelled Sheila over the din. "They're all lined up like sheep."

"Most of them look like sheep, too. Let's just get something to drink," Cathy yelled back. "Like a Coke or a lemon-ade."

"What's a Coke? All you'll get here is a hot cup of tea later with a little slice of cake."

Realizing the slip she'd just made, Cathy lied. "I said cocoa!"

"Later." Sheila pushed her way through the bevy of young girls toward the airmen. "Come on, Cathy, we want the first pick."

"I'm trying to squeeze through."

"Hope they keep playing good music. I love to jive."

"I'm afraid I'm not a good dancer. I've never done jive before."

"You must have lived in a nunnery! Everyone knows how to. It's very popular."

"I'm glad you cleared that up," Cathy answered in a sarcastic tone. The music had stopped, so they could converse in normal voices.

"Hullo, young ladies." The young man's voice came from behind them. They swung around and faced him. "I'm Lieutenant Albert White. Bert, for short."

Cathy was stunned. He held out his hand to her, and she shook it, although she was startled. He looked so like her husband it was a shock. He had the same name, the same blond look and the same blue eyes.

"Pleased to meet you. I'm Cathy White."

"I'll be darned, we have the same last name."

"What a coincidence," she answered, staring at him.

"Mine's been passed down through a zillion generations, though," he said as he returned the gaze.

Cathy felt her face blush. *Why am I so foolish?* He was, as an elderly relative would say, the spitting image of Al, and, of course, of Ed and Alb in her past. She wished all her lives would end. Well, she didn't want her life to end, just the many phases she had passed through lately. When she woke up from this dream—if it were a dream because, at times, it had been a nightmare—she would hold onto Al and never let him out of her sight.

"Ah-hum," Sheila said, interrupting her thoughts.

"Oh, yes. This…is my friend…Sheila Parks," she faltered through her embarrassment.

"Hello, Sheila." Bert held out his right hand.

Sheila did not poke her hand out in friendship. Instead, she said sharply, "Aren't you the nutty blokes who drove by us on the road?"

"Yes, we're the ones," Bert answered with a grin.

"Well, you bloody near killed us. Careening around the roads like you own the place."

"Sorry about that." Bert said—defensively. "Hope our old banger didn't scare you, but you must realize you were out in the road and around a corner. We didn't see you at first."

"You were driving too fast."

"Not me exactly. It was my friend here, Lieutenant John Moore."

John Moore stepped into their circle. He was handsome, with dark hair and eyes, and suddenly Sheila seemed mesmerized.

"Forgive me?" John stuck out his hand to Sheila.

"You're forgiven," Sheila mumbled. With her eyes locked on his, she shook hands with him.

"I'm glad. I would have lost sleep if you hadn't," he teased.

Sheila smiled as her eyes refocused.

"I say, old boy. Don't I get introduced, too?" piped up a mocking voice from behind Bert.

Bert winked at the two girls as he turned to the young man. "Let me introduce you to Lieutenant Harold Lear," he said. He presented the other officer with a mocking flourish of his right arm and a slight bow.

"Pleased, I'm sure," Harold mocked. "I like to meet the local peasants."

"Well, only one sentence out of you, and we know you're someone we don't want to get to know," Sheila retorted.

"Ah-ha, a perfect example of once a peasant, always a peasant," Harold scoffed. "A good argument for negative eugenics."

"That's an ignorant remark." Cathy jumped into the conversation.

"Oh, Miss Clever Dick Know-It-All." He snickered. "Another lowly village maiden?"

"I beg your pardon, Mr. Lear—"

"Lieutenant, not mister, to you," Harold snarled.

"Whatever your name is, that is an ignorant remark to make about a person," Cathy countered.

"What did he mean?" Sheila asked turning to face her friend.

"It means, my dear, peasants breed peasants because they're unintelligent due to genes passed down through the family and should be sterilized or eliminated as being unfit for society."

"Yes...well...er...right," Harold muttered as he looked down at his shoes.

Cathy enjoyed seeing him squirm. *Another little Hitler,* she thought.

"Blimey, how come you're so brainy, Cathy? You're really smart," Sheila gushed, then glared at Harold. "You're scum," she snapped.

Disgusted, she turned her back to him and faced Bert and John. An embarrassing silence fell over the group.

Cathy was trying to think of what to say to change the subject to a lighter subject when Sheila broke the uneasy quiet.

"How on earth do you blokes get the petrol to run around in your car all the time?" she asked the men. "We can't get petrol to run our tractors, let alone for a car, if we had one!"

"You have to know the right people." Bert laughed. "I have an American friend stationed in the motor pool at the Rougham aerodrome, so I can buy all the fuel I need. Within reason, of course. The Yanks have rationing, but at least they have petrol when you need some. Wouldn't want to take advantage, though, and get him into trouble."

"Of course not," Harold Lear piped up behind them. "Honor among thieves."

"Shut up, Harold," Bert mumbled out of the corner of his mouth. "No one asked you for your bloody opinion."

"Well, you've got it, so lump it."

"You're the first one to hitch a ride with us, aren't you? So show some manners and mind your own business."

With a huff, Harold Lear turned on his heel, strode across the room, and joined a group of giggling teenage girls, obviously impressed by his rank.

Although it was not quite dark outside, the bare-bulb electric lights were clicked on. One by one, the blackout curtains were drawn over each window. Thick curtains were pulled over the doorway and across the entryway door. It reminded Cathy of an air lock, but, instead of trapping air, the curtains trapped any escaping light.

The music started again. The old gramophone blared out a Glenn Miller tune and the room came alive with couples bouncing and swinging around to the lively music.

John pulled Sheila out onto the dance floor, or rather to the middle of the room, and they immediately became part of the laughing, jiving, swirling throng.

Chapter 3

"Wanna dance?" Bert asked as he turned his attention back to Cathy. He found her pretty and interesting. Quite the opposite from the other local village girls he had met.

"No, I don't know these dances. Thanks for asking, though."

"I could teach you. You're missing a lot of fun in your life." He smiled.

"Maybe another time. I fell off a farm cart today, and I'm now feeling the bumps and bruises. I'm not as resilient as I used to be." She sat down on one of the chairs lining the wall.

"Getting old?" He laughed and pulled up a chair next to hers.

"I suppose so. I'm no spring chicken…almost thirty."

"Me, too."

Cigarette smoke drifted by from the row of male wallflowers leaning against the wall next to them. Cathy fanned the air in front of her face. "Why don't we go outside for some fresh air? There're some benches on the lawn out there."

"Good idea. It's getting stuffy in here." He extended his hand to her and pulled her to her feet.

They pushed their way through the crowd and over to the interior door where he held back the black curtain for her. Once inside the porch, she pulled back the outside door curtain for him, and they made their way outside.

Except for a half moon shining through some clouds, total darkness surrounded them. In the distance, sirens wailed as spotlights shone on the low clouds. She had to remind herself that the searchlights were playing on incoming German planes, and weren't the advertisement for a new film. The drone of plane engines hung in the air as the ack-ack of ground fire spat tracers and bullets in and among the planes. A bullet hit its target and one of the planes listed crazily onto its left wing and started to spin, around and around, with flames pouring out of its engine, lighting up the sky as it fell like a rock to earth. They heard a thud and the horizon lit up brighter momentarily.

"Another life extinguished." she said quietly. "Hope no one on the ground gets hurt."

"Bloody war. When will it end?" Bert came up behind her and absentmindedly put his arms around her shoulders.

She pushed his arms away. "A little familiar, aren't we?"

"Pardon me. I was lost in thought," he said as he backed away with this hands outstretched. "I wasn't thinking. No need to get huffy."

"Sorry. I didn't intend to insult you. You surprised me with the sudden move."

"Maybe Harold was right about you. You do have a better-than-thou demeanor," he noted, with a touch of sharpness in his voice.

"Touché." Cathy patted the bench next to her. "Sit."

"Woof, woof," he said, while panting like a dog.

"Sorry…again. We seem to have started off on the wrong

foot."

"If you say so." He plopped down on the bench beside her. "Tell me more about yourself. You appear to be well-educated."

"There's really not much to tell of any interest."

"I'll be the judge of that."

"It's just several years of schools, universities, becoming a teacher, et cetera. Dull to you, I'm sure."

"I'd be fascinated. A teacher, eh? I'm a writer—when I'm a civilian anyway. I just had my first-time travel novel published. It's a time-travel back through time. Lots of history in it—the Crusades." He leaned back on the bench.

The couple sat in silence for a moment or two.

* * * *

"Remarkable. We have more in common than you can imagine." She held back. She couldn't divulge her own story just yet.

"Really?"

"I'm working on my dissertation, and it involved much historical research, starting in Anglo-Saxon times."

"Quite a lot of Roman and Anglo-Saxon history background around these parts."

She nodded and then sat silently for a moment.

"Are you married?" she asked.

"No," he said emphatically. "You?"

"I don't think you'll believe me if I tell you."

It had happened again, where she felt compelled to tell her story, even though it was unbelievable. *Why can't I lie?* she asked herself.

"I think I know the answer."

"You do?"

"You're married. You have an untanned white mark

around your ring finger. A dead giveaway. Why are you hiding the fact that you're married?"

"You'd make a good detective," she said. She shifted herself on the seat. "I'm not hiding anything. I lost my ring."

"How long have you been married?"

"I think the best question is to ask me when were you married?"

"Okay, when were you married?"

"April fourth, 1993." She waited for the reaction.

"What? Ninety-three!" he exclaimed.

"Yes, that's correct."

"But it's fifty years from now. Well, I now know you *are* a little potty." He moved away from her, putting space between them on the bench.

"I'm not insane. It's a long story, but the bottom line is I'm from the future. Sixty years from now to be more specific."

"You're ridiculing me because I write time-travel books."

His anger showed on his face. Cathy wasn't sure whether she should continue, but she didn't want to offend him. "Bert, I'm not ridiculing you at all. It's the truth."

"You expect me to believe that cock-and-bull story?" he scoffed. "I wasn't born yesterday. I write time-travel books, but it's imagination. I mold many historical facts into one piece of fiction. It's fantasy. I don't believe that one could really travel back through time. It's ludicrous. Have you seen a doctor about your hallucinations?"

"It's *not* a hallucination. I received a head injury in a car accident and suddenly woke up in Anglo-Saxon times."

She continued to relate her story about how she'd lived two other lives in past history and now lived in here, in 1943. Rehashing the past events drained her emotionally. She was tired, tired of living in strange historical settings, tired of learning to survive, and tired of explaining her lives to skeptics.

He stared at her face in the moonlight. "You look normal," he said, "but I find your story incredulous. It would make a great novel, though. I may write it up someday. That is, if you don't mind being written about." Sarcasm tinged his statement.

"I'm sorry you find me a liar—a story teller," she snapped. Irritated, Cathy stood up, ready to leave and return to the dance. "Everyone who's heard my tale didn't believe it at first, but later on, I proved I wasn't making it up. I'm from the future and I wish I could return to it right now. I shouldn't have told you, but I can't lie. I wish I could." The darkness hid the tears welling up in her eyes, but her voice trembled, almost choking.

"Does Sheila know this?" he asked, almost kindly.

"No, I only arrived here in the village today. It will take a while to find the right time…"

"But you thought you'd tell me, a total stranger."

Strange. I know. It's just that I feel we're connected through time. You look exactly like my husband, Al. His full name is Albert, the same as yours. Don't you see the connection?"

"Maybe I'm his grandfather," Bert mocked.

"Don't joke about this. How do we know you aren't?" she asked as she turned to face him.

"This is too strange," he added. "Are you sure you don't have a mental problem?"

"I'm sure," she said quietly.

"I'll have to think about this. Let's go inside."

Chapter 4

Little Rose spooned small squares of bread with milk and sugar into her mouth, dribbling a lot on her chin. Alice had prepared Cathy's breakfast of two thick slices of bread smeared with beef fat saved from the roast on Sunday—drippings—as Alice described the greasy, though tasty, spread.

"Is there any fruit?" Cathy asked.

"No. Too soon for our apples and no fruit coming into the country. The merchant marine ships didn't get through this week. Our food's feeding the fish at the bottom of the sea…along with the merchant marines. Poor blighters."

It was at times like these that Cathy yearned to return to the twenty-first-century, with its choices of a variety of cereals, yogurt, and fruit for breakfast. She told herself it was a selfish thought. At that moment, this was her real life. Ships being sunk right at this minute. It had happened sixty years ago, but it was also happening in her life right now. If she pinched herself, it hurt. She bled when she grazed her hands in the fields.

Am I in a parallel world? What is real?

"Time I left for work," she called out to Alice.

She slammed the front door closed and stuffed her dripping sandwich in her mouth. She picked up her bicycle that was outside leaning on the bushes next to the garden path. She pushed open the gate to the road, got on her bike, and pedaled toward the nearest farm. It was a lovely day to be out in the countryside.

The weeks had crawled by, moving the seasons with them. Alice had taken her to the borough hall, where Cathy had been issued a replacement ration book, and been accepted into the land army and provided with her uniform.

July had dawned hot with plenty of rain showers. Cathy and Sheila toiled for weeks hoeing the weeds that shot up in the fields of potatoes, sugar beets, and brussel sprouts. The heat sapped the energy from the crops and from them. At the end of each day they were sunburned and exhausted with blistered hands.

The summer sun brought the ripening of the oats to a toasty gold. Fuel for the tractors, which sat rusting in the old barn, was even harder for a small farm to obtain during harvest time. So they had to rely on three heavy working horses to bring in the harvest. Wilson garnered some local farmers as volunteers to assist him in pulling the old horse-drawn binder out of the barn and hitched it to the horses.

Since Wilson was the strongest of anyone on the farm at the time, naturally he took charge of the huge binder. Carefully guiding the horses down the rows of oats, the binder cut the ripe grain, then tied a knot around each bundle or sheave and dumped it on the ground, ready for gathering.

Wilson was known as "Old-Man Wilson," although he was only in his sixties. Cathy and Sheila were totally surprised when Old-Man Wilson's father showed up at the farm to teach them how to stack the sheaves. They dubbed him "Really-Old-Man Wilson." They marveled at the energy of the elder Wilson. He was wiry, with no fat on his wrinkled, slender frame, and he proudly disclosed to them his age as eighty-five years.

"Now watch what oi do here," he warned them in a thick Suffolk accent. "Take holt of between eight and ten sheaves. Thems then called shocks. What you're doing's called stooking when you pile 'em in a pyramid style. Now watch me."

He swiftly gathered up armfuls of sheaves and leaned them against each other into a triangular shape. Then it was their time to try. Cathy loaded up her arms with sheaves, but immediately dropped half the load. Sheila had no problems with her sheaves and laughed and giggled as Cathy struggled. After about fifteen minutes, both girls were stacking the sheaves of grain like they had been born to work building shocks.

"What happens next?" Cathy called over to the senior Wilson. "Does a machine come and pick up the shocks?"

"Yep," he answered, "'cept the machine's got two legs and a pitchfork."

"Sounds like fun," she said sarcastically.

"They dry in the field for about three weeks," Sheila explained. "Then we have to pick up the shocks with a pitchfork and pile it on a cart. It's taken to the grain yard and we build a haystack."

"My back's hurting just listening," Cathy joked.

"Around October, it's then threshed to separate the grain from the straw."

Cathy's eyes were growing larger with each sentence.

"Then we build another stack with the straw. In the

meanwhile, we'll be felling trees, digging ditches, and spreading manure on the fields."

"I don't think I'll survive all the lifting. It's more work than of a stevedore," Cathy confided to Sheila. "How does one get transferred to another job?"

"There's always a dairy farm, where you can get up at four a.m. to milk the cows. Oh, yes, I do know two gals who are rat and mole catchers. Would you like any of those jobs?"

Cathy wrinkled her nose in disgust. "I suppose I'll have to stick with this place. At least I have you to pal around with."

"You poor thing! Let's take a tea break." Sheila linked arms with Cathy and they laughed together as they headed for their Thermos® flasks of tea at the side of the field.

* * * *

Bert and John called them a couple of times a week at the village telephone kiosk at agreed-upon times. If the men had to work, the girls would stuff themselves into the red call-box kiosk, giggling like two schoolgirls, dial O for the telephone operator, and wait for the, "Number, please," followed by instructions.

They'd be told to insert one shilling and six pence for three minutes. The shilling coin would make two "bongs" as it struck a bell, and the sixpence would make one "bong." As soon as Bert or John answered, the operator would tell the girls to, "Please press button A," which they did to make the money fall with a clunk into the money box. They'd then have three minutes to take turns talking, while drawing hearts and arrows on the steamed-up window glass.

On a few Saturday nights they'd all pile into the old jalopy and drive into town to the Odeon in Bury. There, after being checked at the door to see if they had their gas masks with them, they cuddled in the last row of the cinema and watched the latest news on the war and then black and white films—mostly with patriotic wartime themes. One could count on predictable story lines, but the films were enjoyable as they diverted everyone's attention from the hard times surrounding them.

If Bert managed to wangle a Sunday afternoon off duty, he and Cathy would spend the time walking around the old Abbey Gardens in town. They admired the flowers and played a fun game of lawn bowling. Neither of them had much money, but they were happy and free for the few hours they were together. To Cathy, Bert acted exactly like her beloved husband—except Bert was here, now, in this time.

Chapter 5

It had taken more than two weeks to save up the rations for the picnic. On the morning of the outing, Mr. Dorling, the local bread baker from nearby Chimney Mills, delivered an extra loaf of bread with a wink. Cathy sliced up the grey-colored National Flour loaf of bread and spread it with the artificial, yellow margarine. She'd been stingy because, as Alice had reminded her, you only got a quarter of pound a week and you had to make it last. Butter was out of the question—the two-ounces-a-week butter ration was always saved for Sunday teatime. She marveled at how the British survived such restrictions. Excess and wastefulness would be the norm of Western societies in fifty years.

As her donation to the event, Alice generously gave them a small jar of jam.

"I registered at this one shop in Bury for my half-pound of sugar for the week, and each week you get a coupon. When you've got four coupons, you're allowed to buy a jar of jam," she announced, arms folded with some degree of self-satisfaction.

"Thank you so much," Cathy said as she carefully cradled the precious jar in her hands and read the label. "Strawberry.

My favorite."

"Used to be my favorite, too, but the little pips get under my false teeth and hurt like the dickens. Now, I just eat smooth plum jam."

"You're so young to have false teeth."

"Had so many bad teeth, the dentist pulled them out. They don't fuss with fillings during a war." Alice looked embarrassed.

"Sorry. I didn't mean to insult you."

"I know."

So Cathy spread the bread sparingly with the jam, and realizing there was no such thing as foil or plastic wrap, wrapped the sandwiches in a pure-white tea towel. She brewed a big pot of tea with some of her own ration, which she poured into a heavy, metal vacuum flask to keep it hot. *Some chilled white wine, Monterey Jack cheese, veggies and dip, and cheesecake for dessert would really go down well,* she thought. Her stomach rumbled in protest.

The day had dawned with perfect weather. The "Farmer's Daughters," as Cathy and Sheila had named themselves, piled the food and drink on top of the cardboard boxes holding their gas masks into their bicycle baskets, and rode through the village, down a dirt path to the favored spot by the River Lark.

They leaned their bicycles against a large oak tree and looked for a level piece of ground without huge tree roots breaking through the soil and not too many acorns strewn on the ground. They hoped their gentlemen guests could find the place from their directions. There were no road signs—they'd been taken down to foil enemy agents—and so explicit directions were always required.

Warm breezes gently played with the tablecloth and blanket Cathy had spread out in the shade of the leafy tree. She wore a cotton skirt and short-sleeved blouse with shoulder pads. She felt free, like a little girl donning her Easter outfit, with legs freed of winter's heavy trousers and arms freed of itchy sweaters. What a glorious feeling it was.

She remembered her mother, who made her Sunday best clothes with a matching outfit for her favorite doll. She missed her so much. Her eyes watered up, but she resolved to be brave and work through this period in which she lived. When would she get back to her husband and family?

A blackbird sang a glorious, full-throated song, and a cuckoo called out in the nearby woods.

"Have you ever wondered why a cuckoo makes that noise?" Sheila asked.

"It's probably cheering about laying her egg in another bird's nest, and about how the baby cuckoo will throw out the other baby birds so it gets more food."

"So there's really never a cuckoo's nest." Sheila laughed. "There's a story in there somewhere."

"It's a possibility." Cathy smiled inwardly as she laid out the food, plates, and cutlery on the tablecloth. Once done, she settled down on the wool blanket.

A few minutes later, a car horn shattered the peace.

"Sounds like their hooter," said Sheila, jumping up and down like a child.

Beep, beep, beep preceded the rattle, wheeze, and squeak of the springs on the old car bobbling across the meadow. In a cloud of dust, the car came to a halt close to the girls.

"Hello, there!" called Bert while opening the car door and getting out.

Cathy noticed the door opened to the back.

He smiled as he walked over to where Cathy sat and

seated himself cross-legged on the blanket. John Moore climbed out of the passenger's side of the car.

"You found the place all right?" Sheila asked. She ran over to the handsome man and brazenly hooked her arm into his.

"No problem," he answered with a grin. He patted her hand. "It's nice to see you again."

Sheila plopped down on the blanket and tapped the spot next to her. "Sit next to me." She giggled. "Really close."

"Don't have to ask me twice." John laughed and settled down on the blanket behind Sheila and pulled her back to lean on his chest.

"Is everyone hungry?" Cathy asked. She opened the tea cloth to reveal the sandwiches and unscrewed the top of the tea flask. *This is just like a scene in a corny old black-and-white "B" movie.*

"Always," Bert admitted.

"Me, too," Sheila and John said in unison, making them laugh at themselves.

They enjoyed the food, as well as each other's company. They laughed and joked throughout the picnic as though it were a sumptuous feast set on the lawn of an English manor. For a short time, the raging war with blood, death, and destruction was forgotten.

Once done, the dishes, tea flasks and tea towels were loaded into Cathy's bicycle basket ready for the ride home. Sheila and John were enraptured with each and were in a deep conversation.

Bert, lounging on the blanket, stretched his arms and yawned. "Time to go for a walk, before I fall asleep." He got up, held out his hand to Cathy, and pulled her up to her feet. He pulled her with such a force she ended up in his arms. He squeezed her.

"Thanks." She giggled. "I needed a hug today."

"You can count on me...anytime," he said with a laugh. "You're my very own potty professor."

Bert seemed to have come to terms with her story, she thought, but she trusted he wasn't just going along with it, going with the flow, as they say in modern days. She'd give him the benefit of the doubt, though.

He took her hand in his and turned to the other couple. "We're taking a walk down the river toward the bridge. You make sure you go the other way."

"All right, mate." John gave him a wink. "C'mon, Sheila, let's go. We know when we're not wanted."

The couple linked hands and headed off in the opposite direction.

Bert and Cathy strolled along the riverbank, where dragonflies flitted like iridescent rainbows over the river's surface. "You're like one of those dragonflies," Bert said quietly. "You, too, have journeyed through several stages in your life."

"Your observation is so poetic. So sweet of you," she said. They watched the dragonflies in a colorful ballet of swooping and darting over the water. "They're so beautiful," Cathy murmured.

"Not as beautiful as you are," Bert whispered as he pulled her close to him.

"I'm a plain Jane." She looked up at his face as he wrapped his arms around her.

"You are not."

"Yes, I am."

"Not from where I'm standing."

"If you insist," Cathy said quietly as her mouth brushed his.

She closed her eyes. Although they hadn't known each

other long, it felt as though she'd been familiar with him for years. He resembled Al so much. Sometimes the thought that this man may be related to her husband repulsed her. It felt almost incestuous, although she reminded herself it wasn't so. It must be a dream.

She did know she wanted his body next to hers—naked, with his muscles pressing against her bare breasts. He took her face in his hands and kissed her eyelids so softly and as gently as a butterfly alighting on them.

They walked along the footpath until they reached a weeping willow tree. Its branches, thick and leaf-covered, drooped down and touched the ground. Bert parted the branches. "Come into my boudoir," he joked as he held the branches back for her to step through them.

Inside, she looked around. It was like a huge umbrella consisting of bright-green leaves sheltering them and shutting out the dirt of war. The sun dappled through the branches making sun patterns on the ground. It seemed safe from peering eyes inside this bower.

They spread the blanket.

"I want to make love to you," he whispered, his voice husky with lust.

"What? No I-may-be-killed-tomorrow' speech? You *are* very direct."

"No. No coercion. We're both adults and can make our own decisions. So, I repeat, I want to make love to you," he told her quietly.

She gazed into his eyes. *So blue.* "I want you to," she answered with her lips on his, tasting him. "Do you have some protection?" She didn't know if the word "condom" was ordinarily used.

"Yes, I have a French letter," he whispered.

He held her so close. She could feel the tightness of his muscles as his lips moved down to her neck. His body clung to hers, pushing against her pelvis, taut and hard.

Gently, he lowered her down on to the blanket. She could hardly breathe. The only thought in her head was she had to touch his skin. She quickly unbuttoned his shirt, and he pulled it off. His skin was tanned and rippled with muscles as he moved. She kissed him, hard, and rough.

"Please, please," she pled through gritted teeth.

He tugged at her blouse and struggled with the buttons. She sat up to help him remove it. She slipped the blouse off her arms, leaving her naked. He cupped her breasts in his hands, with nipples hard and pert, aroused from his touch, and then kissed each one.

"You don't wear a bra?" he whispered.

"No. I'm a liberated woman."

"A free woman?"

"Yes."

"Nice."

His lips moved between her breasts and kissed her down to her belly. She trembled.

"Cold?"

"No. Don't stop there."

His hand drew an imaginary line down her belly to the depths of her desire. His touch made her explode and she squirmed under his hardness. His breathing was labored as he pulled at her underwear.

"Please, hurry," Cathy whispered.

He fumbled with a small package he pulled out of his wallet. His hands trembled as he dropped the condom onto the blanket.

He drew in a breath through his teeth.

"Relax, darling. Don't get frustrated," she sighed in his ear.

He bolted upright. "Sssh. I heard something rustling in the bushes," he murmured.

Cathy's anticipation of making love dispersed.

They both sat in silence. *Rustle, rustle.*

"Hey, Bertie! What are you doing in there?" The voice crashed into their world.

"It's Harold," Bert groaned. "Get dressed...quick."

He pulled on his pants and shirt before shouting out to the intruder, "What in the hell do you want, Harold? Can't a man have some privacy without you barging in all the time?"

"Just wanted to say hello. Was riding by on my bike and saw your car down in the meadow. Wouldn't want you to think I ignored you."

"I'd rather you ignore me." Bert pulled back the branches, stepped out into the open and looked around for Harold.

He heard a thud like someone had fallen.

"Blast!" Harold cried out. "I think I've sprained my ankle."

"Where are you?"

More cursing ensued.

"Over here. Behind this tree," came the response.

More rustling of leaves and the cursing of all things natural drifted out from behind the tree.

"Damned rabbit holes. They're all over. Ouch! I've sprained my bloody ankle."

Chapter 6

Two evenings later, Bert parked his car near the hedges that fenced in the church's meadow. The gate was locked, only to be opened on Sundays, for weddings, and an occasional funeral. He and Cathy climbed over the wooden stile and linked hands as they strolled along the path leading through the field toward the village church. Dark clouds scudded across the sky, creeping across the face of the moon and then moving on, revealing the full orb, bright and smiling down on earth. Bushes lined the pathway, some tall, casting long, black shadows, and other shorter shadows barely reaching their feet as they walked by.

Bert stopped and took her other hand in his, kissing each finger tenderly. He cupped her face, and kissed her eyelids with his soft lips.

Stabs of desire drove through her and down her legs, which went limp and almost buckled. Gently, his wet lips moved to her lips where they hungrily moved as one. She ran her tongue over his lips. Her body responded, quivering down low in her stomach. His reaction could be felt, urgently pressing against her body. She opened her eyes. She wanted to see his face which so resembled Al's. As she looked at his face, a movement caught her eye, as a shadow shifted in the bushes.

"Bert, stop…look…someone's in the bushes…watching us!"

Bert spun around, his eyes searching the shadows. They stood there, silent, as they held their breath, waiting for any movement.

"There's nothing there, darling. It's probably only a cloud blocking the moonlight," he observed as his shoulders relaxed. "Why don't we sit on the benches in the church's lych gate and talk?"

"That's fine with me. But I'm really spooked, Bert. I know I saw something."

They opened the wooden gate of the roofed structure and sat down on one of the worn benches, cuddling each other close. His uniform jacket smelled lightly of moth balls. *With winter clothes all made out of wool, this country must be overrun with clothes moths,* she thought.

"You smell like moth balls." She giggled.

"Sorry."

"No need to apologize. Every time I smell moth balls, I'll think of you." She snuggled closer to him. "It's so dark out here."

"Nothing to worry about." He rubbed her back and laughed. "I'm here to protect you."

"You could have a cigarette, if you'd like. A light can't be seen in here."

"Trying to give it up," he said.

"Really? I'm glad. They're not good for you."

She heard a rustling in the dead leaves, hidden by the tall weeds behind them.

"Shush. I heard it again! There *is* someone lurking around out there."

She shuddered at the thought of being stalked by who-knows-whom? No one knew where she and Bert had gone, so it wasn't a friend playing a joke on them. *They could be killed and their bodies wouldn't be found for weeks,* she thought. Clinging onto Bert's jacket as they both stood up to look around, her hands trembled and tightened on the material.

"Just hold my hand," he murmured. "I can't move with you holding onto my jacket like this."

"Sorry," she whispered back, letting go of his jacket. They moved as one as she clung closely to his body. They crept around the gate into the cemetery.

"Careful. There's a big hole to your left. Bomb disposal just removed an unexploded bomb from the churchyard."

A tangle of shrubs with creeping ivy grown over the branches, and dense weeds and stinging nettles made it impossible to search the area in the dark.

"No one could be hiding in that mess," Bert noted. "The rustling must've been a rabbit or some other creature."

"Yes, you're probably right," she conceded as they walked back to the bench and sat down.

"Darling, we have to talk." He let out a loud sigh.

She gave him a quizzical look. "You're going to tell me you've found another girlfriend and this is our final tryst?" she joked.

"No. I'm serious. I have to go away for a few days," Bert announced. He kissed Cathy on the cheek.

"For what?"

"I have to go with a team to disarm a bomb on the Suffolk coast. Top secret, so don't ask me any questions. Military Intelligence is involved, too," Bert said in clipped, cryptic sentences.

"Good heavens!" Cathy exclaimed. "That's so dangerous.

Aren't you nervous?"

"No—it's a pretty standard assignment."

"You must be kidding. I'm nervous for you. So much happened on the Suffolk coast."

Cathy stared ahead into the darkness as she ran through the history stored in her head. There were so many facts crammed in there. She was proud of her ability to recall historical facts—especially British history. Her brows knitted as she concentrated.

"It's important to the security of England," Bert stated.

"Of course it is," she answered. "And they've brought in the best men to do the work. Must be big to call in the Military Intelligence team, too."

"I've heard there's land mines set on the beaches," he said, then was silent for a moment.

She said nothing.

"Cathy, if you know something I should know…"

Her brain was packed with historical facts about the war, but she was determined not to divulge any of them. Being a tell-all in the past had caused tremendous problems. She wasn't going to court fate again.

"You tell stories of the past all the time," he accused her, "and now you won't give me an inkling of what I might encounter."

Cathy kept quiet.

"It's obvious you don't care about me. If you did, you'd warn me of any dangers."

"I do care for you. You're being unreasonable. Don't force me to tell you what I know," she said.

"Rumors are that Germans landed and were killed," Bert said quietly. "Is that true?"

"Why are you insisting on me telling you secrets?" Cathy

snapped. "You're not being fair." She stood up and swung her handbag over her shoulder. "You're ticking me off."

"Sorry you think that way, but, if you're a true friend, you'd tell me what I should avoid out there in Shingle Street." He pounded his fists on the back of the bench. "Damn! I don't believe I said that. I shouldn't be talking about this to you."

"I've read all about it," Cathy said.

"Then tell me what you know, damn it!" He sounded angry.

"There's something special about Shingle Street," she said. She turned with her back to him.

"SShh," he hissed. "The job's top secret. No one is supposed to know about it. For God's sake, don't mention that around anyone else. I understand how you know about it, but just keep it to yourself."

She smiled in the darkness. At last he'd accepted she came from the future.

"I don't believe you won't tell me what you know," he said. "I'm disappointed in you. I thought you were fond of me...maybe even love me."

She swung around to face him. "Okay...you made your point. There was an accident out there. Witnesses stated that the government had developed a chemical weapon bomb. Anthrax, some claimed. The government will keep it secret for thirty years. Nothing's ever been proven, so I don't have any more information for you."

"Preposterous," Bert burst out.

"It's known that it was a biological bomb that had—or should I say has—been developed and manufactured. I wouldn't want you injured out there."

She kissed him on the lips and hoped he would take her forewarning seriously.

"Naturally, I don't want to get injured."

"You must be careful of the beach mines."

"Good Lord! Any other happy news for me?"

"You insisted on me telling you," she said.

"I suppose I should be grateful."

The moon peeked out from behind the clouds. Cathy smiled as they linked hands and started back to the village.

Swinging their hands between them, he teased her about being an old maid while he was away on the assignment. Cathy feared for his safety, but forced herself to keep up a calm front.

"I'm working on a pegged rug. I'll have peace and quiet to work on it with you out of the way!" she countered.

"Sounds boring."

"No, it's relaxing..."

"If you say so," he interjected.

"And when you're finished, you have a comfy rug to walk on. Each strip reminds you of the piece of clothing it came from. Like a memory bedspread made out of... What the..."

Both stopped, dead still. Stunned, they gasped as a shadowy figure emerged from the churchyard. It looked like a man running with a limp at a fast pace through the trees and out of sight.

Her heart thudded in her chest—loud enough for anyone to hear, she thought. The beats thumped in her ears, momentarily drowning out all other sounds.

"I *told* you someone was spying on us," Cathy yelled. "Now do you believe me?"

"Yes, I do now. No need to scream at me," he yelled back.

"Did you notice how he ran?"

"With a limp...yes, it registered all right," he answered.

"Didn't that creep, Harold Lear, sprain his ankle a couple of days ago?"

"Why would Lear be out here watching us?" Bert asked.

"Because he's a rat."

Cathy got goosebumps just thinking about being spied upon. She felt violated. Lear should not to be trusted—he was truly contemptible. As a child, he was probably the class snitch, sneaking around corners, listening to the other kids' conversations and then retelling those stories to a teacher.

She could imagine what Lear would do with the juicy piece of information she'd revealed in the darkness. If he told the authorities, both she and Bert were in deep trouble. She could deny saying anything. Or they could argue that the facts were merely suppositions on her part, but how much would be believed was an unknown factor.

"Damn, damn, damn," Bert cursed. He stomped in a circle as he flailed his arms. His eyes were dark with fear. "If Lear overheard our conversation, it could be the end of my career. How do I get into these situations? Why did you tell me those things? This could ruin me. Sometimes I wish I'd never met you."

"Well, thanks! I feel the same way about you sometimes," yelled Cathy as she grabbed the sleeve of his jacket. "Don't panic! Stop jumping around and let's think." Adrenaline pumped throughout her body. The impulse to flee pounded through her veins.

"Let's get back to the car—quickly." He was breathless with fear. "Out of sight."

"You're right," Cathy said, grabbing his hand as they ran.

The moon slid behind a thick cover of clouds. They had to pick their way carefully down the now-darkened path, avoiding rocks and dips. Now wasn't the time to get injured.

The car finally loomed before them, and Cathy quickly opened the driver's door and flumped down onto the old and worn leather seat.

"It may have just been a peeping tom. If we're lucky, that is." Bert flung the rear door open and grabbed the crank. He grunted when he turned the metal handle that he'd inserted below the car's radiator. "Switch on when I say so and pull out the choke."

After a few stiff turns, the engine came alive with a rasping noise. Cathy moved over to the passenger's seat as Bert threw open the car door and tossed the crank handle into the back seat. He crashed and ground the gears of the old car in his hurry to get it moving. At last, the vehicle jerked forward.

"Drive," Cathy ordered. "Let's put some distance between us and, if it was him, Lieutenant Lear."

The old car creaked and groaned as it seemed reluctant to move.

"Come on. Why is the road ahead so dark? Put your foot down," Cathy snapped, now impatient.

"How in the hell am I supposed to go fast?" he snarled. "I have tiny slits in the covers on my lights. And those slits are facing down. No way can I speed anywhere."

"Sorry, I forgot all about the headlights being covered. At least there's a full moon tonight."

"Bloody hell, Cathy, what are you nattering about now?"

"Just trying to be positive, that's all," she countered.

"Well, at times like these, it's *very* annoying," he growled as he hit the steering wheel with the flat of his hand. Anger welled up into his voice. "War times stink. I hate the fighting. Nothing's simple in life any more."

Bert leaned forward over the steering wheel, peering out at the dimly lit surface ahead of them. The car crawled along the winding, country road. As they rounded a sharp curve, the moon popped out from behind a cloud and brightened up the area. The silhouette of a bicycle jiggled around in front of them.

"Good Lord!" Bert snapped. "What next? It's a bloody obstacle course."

"Go really slow," Cathy instructed as she touched his arm. "It's a serviceman on that bike."

"So?"

"So, see who it is. If it's Lear, we'll turn off at the lane down the road. Then he won't get a good look at us."

"But he's already seen us at the churchyard."

"It's his word against ours. We can always deny ever being there."

Bert drove closer to the cyclist. The man wobbled violently and turned his head to see how close the car was to him. He then stuck out his right hand and waved for their car to pass him.

As he turned his head, the outline of his profile lit up in the moonlight. To the couple in the car, it seemed to burn into their memories.

"Oh, good Lord," Bert spat as he recognized the face, "Just as we expected, it *is* Harold Lear."

Chapter 7

The day was warm and sunny, with no soaking rain, so Cathy had finished her hedge trimming and left Wilson to weave the cuttings back into the hedge, which would reduce the wind whipping through the field in the winter. She walked back to the cottage along a footpath through the neighboring meadow. She saw her landlady first, who waved and then ducked down out of sight. Cathy's eyes widened in curiosity when she approached the cottage's garden gate.

A huge parachute had been spread out over the lawn, overflowing onto the gooseberry bushes and cabbages. Alice and her sister, Edith, who lived next door through the vegetable garden, were attacking the diaphanous blob with scissors, cutting strips about three feet wide.

"What on earth are you doing?" Cathy asked.

"Cutting up a parachute," Edith stated matter-of-factly.

"Well, the kiddies watched a German airman parachute into the sandpit down the road and they ran down there," Alice explained.

"We didn't know about it at the time," interrupted Edith, "or else we wouldn't have let them go. He could've shot them."

"But he didn't, did he?" Alice continued with a question—the usual Suffolk custom. "Instead, he pulled the chute into a bundle, saluted them, and ran away."

"Amazing. How did they get it home? It must weigh a ton."

"They dragged it, but it started to tear, so they came and got us to help," Alice said.

"It'll make several petticoats and blouses," Edith explained. "It's real silk. We won't need it all, so we'll share it with the family. Would you like some?"

"Thanks, no," Cathy answered. "Silk makes me itch."

"Pity." Edith tsk-tsked to show her dismay.

The women bent over and continued to slice the fabric, then rolled it into manageable lengths.

"You're home early, love," Alice noted, not looking up from her project. "Done for the day?"

"Yes, we finished our jobs early because of the dry weather. Also, Wilson took on some Ukrainian refugees to help with the fieldwork. They're taking a lot of the load off us girls. They're nice, but they don't speak a word of English, so we have to pantomime what we want them to do."

"So what are you going to do for the rest of today?" Edith piped up.

"Bert's supposed to come over to see me later on." She wished she could confirm his plans.

The lack of telephones frustrated her. Important news arrived with a dreaded knock on the front door in the form of a telegram. Just looking at the envelope would cause emotionally strong people to quake and feel faint. Telegrams only brought bad news, or so it seemed.

"Ooh, sounds like it's getting serious," Alice said as she

stood up and rubbed her knees. "You've been meeting him quite often lately. Maybe we'll be hearing wedding bells soon."

Cathy's cheeks blushed slightly. "Not likely. He seems to be a career man and, until this war is over, we don't want to make any commitments."

"Shame...but then again, it's sensible. So many local girls are getting married to their sweethearts, but fool around with other men as soon as he's called up for service." Alice shook her head. "Sinful it is."

Cathy hoped her guilty look wouldn't give her away. Here she was, a married woman—albeit in the future—and she had a boyfriend.

Alice rubbed her back. "Just have to hang out the wash on the line, then we're going to ride our bikes and go deal appling. Why don't you come along?" she asked as she gathered up the rolls of silk.

Cathy had no idea what "deal appling" involved, but, since Bert wouldn't arrive at the cottage for a couple of hours, if then, she said she'd like to go with them.

They soon had all of the laundry pegged on the clothesline. Alice stuck the wooden prop, made out of a long forked branch, in the middle of the line to give it more height. Edith wheeled her bicycle from the side yard of the cottage, while Alice strapped her toddler into the chair seat mounted on the back of her bicycle. Cathy pushed her bicycle from the backyard shed and met them outside the garden gate.

The three women rode down the country road for about a mile and then turned onto a lane. It turned out to be the same lane Cathy and Bert had ducked down after spotting Harold Lear on his bicycle. Just thinking about it gave Cathy chills.

They arrived at a clearing and leaned their bicycles against the pine trees. Those were deal pines, Alice explained, and the "deal apples" were pine cones, sticky with resin, used as flammable fire starters in the coal stoves each morning. They soon filled three potato sacks with the pinecones.

The sacks were loaded in the large baskets strapped to their bike handlebars, and Rose was deposited and bound into her bicycle seat. Just then, they heard a loud, growling sound in the distance, accompanied by the wailing of sirens.

"We'd better make a run for it," Alice yelled. "Planes coming—and they aren't Spitfires."

The women pedaled as fast as they could to Alice's cottage.

"No time to get down in the garden bomb shelter. Quick! Under the stairs!" Alice put down her bicycle stand with her foot to keep the bike upright and struggled with the belt holding Rose into her seat on the back. "Success!" Alice said as she picked up the child in her arms. Cathy dumped her bike on the ground and opened the front door. They ran over to the stairway. Edith held the triangular-shaped door open for the others who bent low under the stairs into the hiding hole. *Shades of Harry Potter,* she thought as she crawled into the space covered in thin mattresses.

"I feel safer under the stairs than in the outside shelter," Edith said.

Thump—thump—thump. The sound of heavy bombs could be heard dropping onto the targets near their village.

"They're trying to hit the sugar beet factory," Alice announced.

"Not hit it yet, though," Edith stated.

"Surely they're all not trying to bomb the factory, are they?" Cathy asked.

"No. They're also trying to blow up the dozen or so aerodromes surrounding us. Yanks' as well as Brit bases. Sometimes I feel like we're a bloody target in the middle of it all." Alice sniffed.

They sat in the space, shoulder-to-shoulder, not speaking. The child sucked her thumb and stayed silent. After about ten minutes, the air became stuffy.

"I'm going outside to see what's going on," Alice announced as she picked up her child and parked her on her hip. "The planes don't sound like they're near us."

"We'll all go," Edith said.

They crawled out of the makeshift shelter and went outside to watch the nine or ten planes circling the area. Anti-aircraft guns, or ack-ack guns, manned by the older village men in the home guard were shooting at—and missing—the enemy planes.

Most of the planes had already dropped their loads and were circling in preparation of returning to their home base across the North Sea. Cathy shielded her eyes and watched the planes overhead. A bomb on one of the planes had not been properly released and, in order to dislodge it, the pilot "waggled" the plane's wings and successfully jettisoned the bomb.

"Good heavens," Alice cried out. "Looks like that bomb landed near the church."

"Didn't go off neither," Edith said.

"No church tomorrow," Alice announced to the group. "Bomb disposal takes ages lately."

"Well, they've gone. Gotta go home now and cook tea for Ted," Edith said. She picked up her bicycle and bag of pine cones.

"On home guard patrol?" Alice asked.

"On the job, but not patrolling."

"Where is he then?"

"Promise you won't get all teary-eyed?" Her blue eyes were misty.

"Me? Teary-eyed? Never," Alice blustered.

"All right then. He and some other blokes had to ride into Bury and unload some lorries. They were full of fold-away cardboard coffins. In case we get blitzed."

"I'm sorry I asked," Alice confessed. A stray tear rolled down her cheek.

Chapter 8

The wind whipped open Cathy's Macintosh raincoat, or "mac" as it was commonly called. Rain pelted her face like tiny darts. She pulled her mac closed and tugged on the belt buckle to tighten it. She crammed her rain bonnet further down on to her head.

A man walked briskly toward the bus stop. He touched the peak of his trilby as a greeting to her. The hat brim was pulled down low putting his face in the shadow, and his hands were buried in the pockets of his trench coat with the collar turned up against the rain. *Creepy,* she thought. *He looks like a villain in an old-fashioned mystery story.* She chuckled to herself. Her imagination had gone haywire lately.

Just then, the bus chugged down the road toward her. The eastern counties bus was a bright red-and-cream with no upstairs. Once she was aboard, the bus rattled along the country road, so she steadied herself by holding tightly onto the handrail as she made her way to an empty seat in the middle of the bus. The mystery man sat in the last seat staring straight ahead.

She placed her wicker shopping basket by her feet and

unbuttoned her raincoat. *What a lousy, cold, rainy, day. No won-der the British have fought everyone who looked at them cross-eyed. It must have been the bone-chilling cold that made them so contentious.*

She wiped her hand in a circle on the steamed-up window so she could see the sweet cottage gardens stuffed with color-ful and dewy-wet flowers, trailing swags of roses draped over small, wooden doors.

"Tickets?" chirped the female bus conductor. Before leav-ing the house, Alice had asked her to say hello to the "clippie," Evelyn.

The conductor lurched down the aisle, leaning her behind on the seat backs as she clipped return tickets and called out, "Tickets, please." Her face was framed with brassy blonde hair swept up off her face with combs, topped with a navy, shiny-peaked uniform hat sitting at a tipsy angle. She held a paper punch in her right hand.

"'ullo, love," she sputtered through several gaps in her teeth as she took Cathy's ticket and clipped a hole in it.

"Hello. Are you Evelyn?"

"Yeah, who're you?"

"I'm staying at Alice Frost's."

"Oh, ah. Been there long?"

"Not very long. She says 'hello' to you."

"Ta, love. Tell 'er likewise," Evelyn said, as she moved down the aisle to handle the other passengers.

Head-scarved countrywomen climbed onto the bus at each stop. Buxom women with large, childbearing hips and rosy, wind-burned cheeks. Each toted a large wicker basket to fill with the week's provisions of tea and lard and whatever slab of meat was available. Shaking the rain off their head-scarves, each made her way to an empty seat, holding onto the overhead handrail while the bus jerked with each change of gears.

Cathy admired these women who lived in this microcosm she knew would drive her insane. She knew she wouldn't be satisfied to just live in a little village with a war raging, no social life, rationed food, rationed clothing, no TV, few telephones, no mobile phones, and no Internet. She wished she could return to the future. Or was it the present? Her head ached just thinking about the life she'd been forced to live.

Belching out diesel fumes, the bus made its way by the Flempton church with the pub almost in its backyard. Across the street, the blacksmith, clad in a tough leather apron, held a horse's foot between his knees as he nailed on a new horse shoe. Ironically, the blacksmith's shop sat in the shade of a large horse chestnut tree.

"Under a spreading chestnut tree, the village smithy stands." She quoted the words of Wordsworth under her breath.

At the Hengrave village stop, an elderly man in a tweed suit and cap stashed a wooden crate of homing pigeons in the luggage compartment near the door.

"Railway station, please," the man piped up to the conductor as he slid into the first seat. The large manila label tied on the crate with string told the story: National Pigeon Service, followed by a London address.

"They're going to the war effort," continued the man to whoever happened to be listening. "Birds like these here carry messages from the war fronts to headquarters." The sleek birds looked innocuous. They cooed and fluttered in the crate, which was headed to the war. These small, feathered creatures were destined to be among the many unsung animal heroes of the war.

The bus ambled along the winding village roads. It chugged by squat, Norman-built churches and thatch-roofed cottages wearing garlands of roses around their doors. In one village, people scuttled along the walks, heads down against the rain, toward the tiny local grocery shop. Neat piles of green cabbages, red-skinned potatoes, and orange carrots vied for attention outside the shop, while colorful flowers in steel buckets lined the shop's doorway.

The pigeon owner was dropped off with his crate of birds at the bus stop outside the pub at the bottom of the Station Hill. Finally, the bus reached the town of Bury St. Edmunds and chugged up Northgate Street, swayed on the sharp right turn onto Looms Lane, and parked at the bus station.

Cathy waited for the chatting women to disembark before she got up from her seat. The "mystery" man had disappeared among the shoppers. She pulled her raincoat belt tight, tucked her basket handle into the crook of her arm and stepped down off the bus.

She then walked behind the town's museum, Moyses Hall, and up Brentgovel Street to the corner butcher's shop. A long queue of people snaked down the narrow sidewalk from the shop's doorway. Cathy cursed under her breath— she'd have to wait ages that day. She joined the end of the line and hoped some meat and sausages would still be left when she got up to the counter. Rationing was bad enough, but when the supply ran out, it became a minor disaster.

The rain stopped and the umbrellas in the queue were closed, shaken over the gutter, and rolled up. Sunshine struggled through the dark clouds.

"Well, dear," a woman piped up to her companion, "they

stretch the meat supply whenever they can. This butcher mixes so many breadcrumbs in his sausages you don't know whether you should put jam or mustard on them." Several people chuckled and concurred it was funny, but true.

"You also have to keep your eye on 'em when they weigh your order. I've caught 'em with a finger on the weights on the scales," another huffy woman added.

Cathy looked around. Her breath caught in her throat. *There he is again!* The man from the bus leaned nonchalantly on a wall about fifty feet away. His hat still shadowed his eyes, so she couldn't be positive that he was watching her in particular. He puffed on a cigarette and blew the smoke out in rings. She believed he saw her, but then maybe it could be a coincidence, but maybe not. *Who is he and what's he doing?*

Her wait in the line wasn't long because each person was restricted to one pound of meat or sausages. Cathy soon moved up level with the shop window where a few white, black-chipped, enameled metal plates held pork chops, liver, and sausages. Once inside the butcher's shop, complete with a sawdust-covered floor, she purchased the one pound of pork sausages on Alice's list and placed them in her shopping basket.

The grocery shop near the post office was next on the list. She glanced at the reflections of the mysterious man in the shop's window. He turned his head and began to walk in her direction. Cathy quickly walked around to the front of Moyses Hall and onto the Cornhill. *Perhaps she could lose him in the crowd,* she thought. It was Saturday and market day, as every past Saturday had been for centuries in the town.

The Cornhill, and the adjoining town square, the Buttermarket, were full of stalls from which vendors hawked anything from vegetables straight from the farm, to brushes, baskets, and flowers. Each stall consisted of a cart or a wooden table protected from the elements by a canvas awning slung between poles at each corner.

She wove in and out of the crowd of shoppers, until it appeared that the man had either lost track of her or wasn't following her after all. Cathy breathed a sigh of relief. It began to drizzle rain again.

She walked briskly through the maze of stalls and wound her way through the market square. Looking to see if any cars were coming, she crossed the street to Boots, the chemist shop occupying a mock Tudor building, and then down a couple of shops and by the post office to a grocery store.

A huge sign reading Maypole hung on the brick wall above the entrance. The shop window, painted a lavatory green, included a few empty cheese boxes, some packages of tea, and a couple of faded boxes of biscuits. In the middle of the window sat a placard issued by the Ministry of Food reminding the reader of each person's weekly allowance of food.

The door was propped open, which allowed a few errant flies to gain access and land on the big wheels of cheese on the counter. There were only two customers in front of her, so Cathy whiled away her wait looking at the shelves full of packages of tea.

"Next!" yelled out the elderly store clerk. He wore a white paper hat balanced on his short, white hair and wiggled his reddish mustache in a nervous twitch.

"I'm next," Cathy answered as she held up her shopping list.

"Yes, madam, what can I get you?"

"Six ounces of Typhoo tea, six ounces of lard, and a half-pound bag of self-rising flour, please," she said, while thinking it seemed hardly enough for three people to live on.

The clerk weighed up the order. He dumped the scoop of tea leaves into a brown paper bag, the flour into another, and then wrapped the lard in greaseproof paper.

"Anything else, darlin'?" he asked. "We have some nice cheddar cheese. Ration went up to eight ounces this week."

She looked into her change purse and counted her money. "Sounds good. Yes, I'll take eight ounces."

The clerk pulled the wire cutter through the large chunk of orangey cheese and cut off a small wedge, weighed it, and wrapped it in paper. Cathy handed him the ration books, and he cut out the appropriate coupons.

"Anything else today, dear?" He handed her the cheese and ration books.

"No, that will be it for today, thank you," Cathy answered as she put the items in her basket. As she exited the shop, she glanced at the line of buildings across the street to her right. She thought she'd seen the strange man standing outside of Croasdale's, the pharmacy, but only women gathered around a baby's pram were there. Although the man looked sinister, she'd determined to put the matter out of her mind and to end her paranoia.

Cathy had about thirty minutes to spend before the bus left to return to Lackford. She decided to look around the town center and some of the shops.

A high-helmeted policeman, with hands linked behind his back, mingled in with the crowd, watching for any spivs operating illegal "black market" activities. Newspaper cartoons she'd seen depicted the stereotypical spiv who wore loud suits, a snappy trilby hat, and had a narrow, pencil-thin mustache. Stolen goods such as silk stockings and food were easily available, as long as you had the money to buy them.

The stalls were lined up decked out with striped awnings like summer deck chairs on the beach. Fresh vegetables from local farms were artfully displayed on many, with vendors peddling their wares. She managed to get a small packet of saccharin from one. It was bitter but better than nothing when the sugar supply ran out.

"Ripe, juicy tomatoes here!" a man yelled from one stall.

"Here, darlin', squeeze these. Nice and firm, ain't they?"

"Get your cukes here."

"Luvly and crisp celery here, ladies. Straight from the fen district," one yelled, referring to the black soil found in the boggy area lying some miles northwest of the town.

Cathy couldn't resist the smell of the celery and bought one still damp from the farm.

She wandered down the market place, and window-shopped at Pretty's, where mannequins in the latest short dresses with big shoulder pads gazed back at her with vacant eyes. The rain stopped and the sun peeked out of the clouds flooding the scene with bright rays.

Cathy pulled off her rain hat and fluffed her hair in the reflection of a shop window. The clock on the old Moyses Hall chimed at the half hour. The bus would leave in about ten minutes.

She had enjoyed her little foray into town, though, and had found the getaway from the farm refreshing.

She walked by Marks and Spencers. The window display held utilitarian cardigans and old-fashioned, long-legged underpants. Warm knickers for the winter—4 coupons the sign announced. With only sixty-six coupons for clothing a year, four coupons for a pair of those knickers wouldn't allow a gal to have too many pairs. Lots of rinsing them out at night with yellow soap and then drying them on the fire fender, hoping they didn't get scorched.

She reached the bus station, found her bus already there and waiting, and seated herself in the same seat area again. Several of the women who came to town on the incoming bus were also on this return trip. She looked around at the passengers. The mysterious man hadn't appeared. She breathed a sigh of relief and settled into the seat. The bus engine started and the bus moved out of its parking spot.

Ding. The conductor hit the bell button with her finger to stop the bus. "Someone's running to catch us," the conductor explained.

Cathy looked out of her window only to see the mystery man running, and jumping onto the bottom doorstep as he swung on the steel handrail onto the bus. Ding, ding. The conductor hit the bell twice to tell the driver to go again.

Damn, it's him. Her heart pounded and she stared straight ahead, not wanting to meet the man's eyes. She thought she'd act as though nothing was wrong, but surreptitiously turned her head slightly sideways so she could glance at him through her peripheral vision.

He stared straight at her.

The ride back to Lackford seemed interminable, but they finally arrived at her stop. As the bus slowed down, she rose and walked past the man toward the exit. *A phone would be handy right then,* she thought. She'd call Bert and tell him about her fears and how this man appeared to be trailing her.

She stepped down off the bus and glanced over her shoulder. The man had got off, too, but walked the opposite direction up the road. *Wonder where he's going?*

The cottage sat snuggled into its flower garden with smoke curling out of the brick chimney. She was glad to be home, even if it was only her temporary home. There'd be Alice to share her story with and calm her nerves over a steaming cup of sweet tea.

Maybe it would make more sense after she'd discussed it with Alice. Cathy shrugged her shoulders. There was nothing she could do to change the events of the day.

Chapter 9

Shadows flashed across the lace-curtained living room window. Cathy and Alice had just finished washing the Sunday dinner dishes and had settled down to read the newspaper.

"Who's that? Someone just went by on the path," Alice said as she jumped up and pulled the curtains back. "Well, it's not the parson." She craned her neck to get a better view. "I can see a man in a mac, one in an overcoat, and someone in...good gracious...it's a police constable! It's Constable Stands."

At that moment there came serious pounding, not a friendly knock, on the door. Cathy walked over and opened the door. There stood the uniformed Constable Stands from the Suffolk Constabulary with two other men. One of his companions was the mysterious man who had followed her in town. Cathy gasped. They were all tall, so the small eighteenth-century doorway cut off their heads from view. They ducked down to be in her line of vision. She noticed a long black car parked at the curb outside of the cottage gate.

What do they want? Her heart pounded. It felt as though it would leap out of her chest. Her hands trembled.

"May we come in, madam?" the policeman said in an officious manner. "I'm Constable Stands of the Suffolk Police, this is Officer Butcher of Scotland Yard, and this is Agent Golledge of Military Intelligence. We have a few questions to ask you."

He stepped down into the living room without waiting for an invitation to do so, and took off his high helmet and tucked it under his arm. The man in the raincoat, Agent Golledge, also came in and removed his hat. He was completely bald, shaved bald, with a dark shadow where his hair had been. The hatless Scotland Yard officer followed them in the door.

"What can I do to help you?" Cathy asked in a confident manner, although inside she quaked with fear. Policemen always made her nervous—even when she wasn't doing anything wrong. Now she feared that her knowing too much about the future had caught up with her. It had happened in the past; there she was, a stranger introduced into a town, but aware of all of its history. She had become conspicuous and raised suspicions.

"Won't you have a seat?" She pulled out chairs from the table. The policeman perched on the edge of a chair as though he were ready to flee.

"I prefer to stand," announced the bald man. He put his hat on the chair seat.

"Need me spectacles," Constable Stands said while he patted his breast pocket from which he pulled out a pair of wire-rimmed eyeglasses. He perched these on the end of his nose. He cleared his throat and shuffled through his small notebook, then licked his index finger and flicked more pages. He stopped at one page and raised his head in order to peer through the glasses, focusing on his scribbled words. He shifted his behind back on the chair and unbuttoned his tunic, obviously uncomfortable with his assignment.

Agent Golledge sighed impatiently. Seeing the constable taking his time, he slapped his hand down on the table. "It appears that our good constable here is unprepared. Typical of the force," he snapped.

"I'll take over, Constable," Officer Butcher said as he rocked back and forth in his black wingtip shoes and looked bored. The policeman sniffed, but trained his eyes on his notebook. Seemingly absorbed, he didn't look up at either man.

"We really only need to confirm your name and some personal information at this juncture," Officer Butcher snapped in a north country accent. He waved his identity card in front of Cathy. "Scotland Yard" was all she could determine before he snatched it from under her nose and stuffed it quickly into an inside breast pocket.

Cathy felt that his demeanor was malevolent as he sucked in his breath through teeth that screamed for dental work. He stuck his hands deep into the pockets on his overcoat, while he continued to rock back and forth on his feet.

Confused, Cathy wondered what the British Military Intelligence and Scotland Yard wanted with her.

"What is your full name?" asked Officer Butcher in the usual brusque, stereotypical, Scotland Yard manner.

Meanwhile, the befuddled constable had his pencil raised to catch every word she said, in writing.

"Catherine Ann White."

"Are you married?"

"Yes."

"Where is your husband?"

"It's a long story."

The men exchanged glances and then back at her.

"Your maiden name then?"

"Hayes."

"Spell it, please."

"H-A-Y-E-S."

"Date of birth?"

She had to lie. These two wouldn't believe she was from the future. Quickly she subtracted her age, twenty-nine, from the date of the year.

"May sixteenth, 1914." *That sounds so far back in time.*

"Place of birth?"

"Great Barton. Near Bury St. Edmunds."

"We're aware of where Great Barton is, miss. No need to embroider your answers," the constable butted in. He licked the end of his pencil.

"Where did you live before you became employed as a land army girl?" the officer continued.

What should she tell him now—another lie? It all became too much for her to bear. She could not continue to make up more stories, but no one would believe her if she told them she'd come from the future. Her heart seemed to skip a beat, and she became faint as the blood drained from her head. Dizziness and nausea tried to take over. Cathy fought back both feelings as she struggled to her feet.

"What is it you want?" she said.

"We need you to come to the station with us, madam," the flustered policeman said. "More questions need answering." He was noticeably embarrassed to insist that a local villager must accompany him to the station house, answer some ridiculous questions, only to be delivered back to the village a few hours later.

"What sort of questions—" Cathy looked over at Alice, who shrugged her shoulders in response.

"You'll see when we get there," interrupted the bald man as he gathered up his hat.

"I need my shoes. They're upstairs."

"You stay here. Madam," he said and turned to Alice, "please be so kind and retrieve Miss White's shoes."

"Afraid I'll make a break for it out of the bedroom window?" Cathy sneered. *This is beginning to sound like a pulp magazine story.*

"Can't be too careful."

A white-faced Alice delivered the shoes to her.

"Don't worry, dearie," she murmured as she helped Cathy put on her shoes. "I'm sure it must be a mistake."

Cathy took her raincoat off the clothes hook next to the door and slipped it on as she followed the agent and officer through the doorway. The constable caught up with them.

Chapter 10

The police car pulled alongside the curb outside the Bury police station. On the opposite side of the street, St. John's Church loomed ominously, with turrets and flying buttresses silhouetted against the evening sky. A steady rain fell onto the empty and dark street.

The men assisted Cathy out of the car, making sure she didn't hit her head as she exited. The agent and officer each took hold of one of her arms and guided her up the worn stone steps, through the frosted glassed double doors into the old-fashioned police station.

At the high wooden counter, the Scotland Yard officer handed over a sheaf of papers to the desk sergeant.

Constable Stands followed them in and removed his helmet.

"Thank you for your assistance, constable. We'll take it from here," the agent said. He shook hands with the elderly policeman.

"We have a few questions to ask this young lady, so buzz us through, please," the officer said to the policeman peering over his eyeglasses at the men who were removing their outer coats. The desk sergeant hit a button on the desk top.

The wooden gate next to the desk clicked open. They pushed through the gate, varnish sticky and dirtied by hundreds of hands pushing it open.

"Follow me," said the agent who preceded Cathy through the gate. The Scotland Yard officer followed her down a hallway. Her damp leather shoe soles slipped on the shiny, dark-brown linoleum. The officer squeezed her arm, which he held to steady her on the slippery floor. He guided her down the hallway and into a small room. He flipped the light switch and a bare bulb spread a dim illumination over a metal table and four metal chairs.

"Have a seat," the agent said brusquely. He pulled out two of the chairs. Cathy sat on one chair, and he sat down on another. The Scotland Yard officer pulled out another chair for himself and straddled it as he leaned on the chair back and stared at her with his icy-blue eyes.

"How come you've never taken your weekend off every six weeks like all of the other girls?" The officer spat the words at her.

Cathy jumped. She wasn't ready for the suddenness of the question. She stared ahead with a blank expression as she tried to collect her thoughts.

Irritated, the officer banged his fist on the table. "As a land army girl, you're entitled to a free railway warrant to travel home, but you've not done that. Where is your family?"

Cathy quickly collected her thoughts. *What to tell them?* She must come up with a plausible answer. She wished she'd concocted that part of her heritage before, when she'd had more time. *Think!* she told herself. *Come up with some place difficult to reach.* She racked her brain. *Come on...okay, I have an idea. No, pleading amnesia wouldn't work because there'd be even more questions into my background.*

"My mother lives on the Isle of Man. It takes more time than a weekend to get there, so I don't visit her," she blurted out.

"We don't believe you," the officer snapped back.

"Well, it's the truth."

"The Ministry of Agriculture has no record of you."

"You must not have looked too hard. I didn't join at the main office in London, you know. I signed up at the Bury Borough Hall." Cathy's heart pounded against her chest. She was sure the men could see it beating through her blouse.

"We'll look into that again, young lady. We've also checked with the Registrar of Births in town. There was no Catherine Hayes born on May 16th, 1914."

"I don't understand why…unless the doctor failed to register me. They did that back then. Sometimes mislaid their list when they went to the registrar's office."

"Too many excuses. Too many lies is more like it."

"If I tell you where I'm really from, will that help?" She wrung her hands. What would she to do now? She was in serious trouble now.

"Maybe. Why didn't you tell the truth to start with?" the officer asked.

"Forget about where's she's from." The military intelligence agent jumped into the interrogations. "How did you obtain the information on Shingle Street when it is top secret?"

She stared straight ahead.

"How do you know there's a secret bomb in development? Who are you working for?"

"I can answer all of your questions if you give me a chance."

"Whoa! You acknowledge that you have information. We don't want any answers yet," the agent said.

"Save it until you get representation and then you can tell it to the judge," the Scotland Yard officer said as he got up from his chair and kicked it under the table. "You'll be heard first thing tomorrow here at the magistrate's court. Then you'll probably be remanded to Holloway Prison in London to await your trial."

"What? You can't do this. What am I being accused of?" she screamed. Panic shook her body. She shuddered as she became ice cold. Holloway Prison was a feared prison, built like a red-bricked castle.

"You're being held in accordance with the *Official Secrets Act*," the officer said quietly.

They think I'm a spy. No one is going to believe my story. I'm finished now. Deserted by everyone. Who could have reported these things? It had to be Harold Lear. He was the only one who heard, or rather overheard, her telling Bert about Shingle Street and the other historical facts.

Could it have been Bert? Maybe he had been stringing her along all the time, just waiting for the right time to inform Military Intelligence. *If only Al were here to get me out of this nightmare. Why can't I escape this time period and go home?* Disheartened, Cathy folded her hands on the table. She then put her head down on her hands as hot tears filled her eyes.

Chapter 11

"Here, Mrs. White," sneered the policewoman as she threw a copy of the local newspaper into Cathy's cell, "something to read as you're waiting to be transported to London. We leave in an hour."

Cathy swung her legs over the side of the hard, thin mattress that served as the bed in the cold and draughty cell. Every muscle hurt from the tension she was under. Sleep had evaded her all night; her day in court had drained her of all emotions. She'd been arraigned.

I'm a criminal. This is a horror story.

She was so alone. No one had been permitted to visit or contact her, not even Sheila. She'd already been told that Harold Lear was the witness for the Crown, and that Bert had also been arrested, so she didn't expect to see him ever again. The Military Intelligence agent had returned to London to retain his anonymity. Cathy felt deserted and betrayed.

"Is it possible to have a shower? I need to freshen up," she called out to the policewoman.

"No. Not possible. You can wash in the sink in your cell. You'll have *plenty* of time to shower when you get to Holloway."

"I'm sure I will," Cathy snapped back.

"Except you'll be watching your back at the same time. Holloway's a difficult prison, with some very tough women inside."

The policewoman walked over to a rust-blotched, painted locker on the opposite wall. She took a bunch of keys and tried several in the locker keyhole until one opened the door with a clunk. The woman rummaged through the contents and pulled out several items, which she handed to Cathy through the cell bars.

Cathy looked down at the pile consisting of a small white towel, a used piece of soap, a toothbrush, and a small, folded piece of paper. "What's in the paper?" she asked.

"Tooth powder. Enough for one cleaning. Tastes like peppermint, which is better than bicarbonate of soda."

Cathy wrinkled her nose. "This is used soap."

"It's war-time. Be happy you have it."

With a sigh, Cathy walked over to the chipped sink against the wall and turned on the hot water. The water ran but it never got hot. Resigned to washing in ice-cold water, she soaped up her face and splashed it with the running water. The coldness went through her body like a steel dagger. The chill made her more determined to be strong, to persevere, despite the hatred directed at her.

She scrubbed her teeth with the wet toothbrush dipped in the powder. It did taste like peppermint after all. She dried her face with the scratchy towel and ran her hands through her hair. There was no mirror—too dangerous the policewoman had told her—so she couldn't check her appearance.

Her clothes were all rumpled from sleeping in them anyway, so she shrugged her shoulders in resignation. *This was as good as she could look,* she thought as she perched on the hard bed, the only item to sit on in the whole cell. She heard a radio in the distance; the music of a flute floated through the police station. A few stray tears ran down her face as she listened to the melody and memories of Al, Ed, and Alb came flooding back.

She picked up the newspaper.

Land Army Gal Is A Spy! screamed the headline on the front page of the newspaper. Under it sat a photo of Cathy, in handcuffs, as she was being led out of the court at the Shirehall in Bury St. Edmunds. She read,

> *The Suffolk Police, in cooperation with the Scotland Yard Special Branch and the Military Secret Intelligence Service, took a local Land Army girl, Catherine White, into custody last evening.*
>
> *White appeared at the Bury St. Edmunds Magistrates' Court this morning where she was arraigned and charged with probable treasonable activities under the* Official Secrets Act. *She has been remanded to custody at the women's jail, Holloway, in North London to await a trial in the near future at the Central Criminal Court (Old Bailey).*
>
> *White has been lodging with Alice Frost in the village of Lackford, about six miles from Bury St. Edmunds. Mrs. Frost stated that she was shocked to hear the allegations against White. "She seemed so normal. Like an innocent country girl," Mrs. Frost said to this reporter.*
>
> *Likewise, White's friends say they are stunned in disbelief at the news.*
>
> *"She's just a working woman trying to make it*

through these hard times," said co-worker, Sheila Parks. "She was always around. She didn't even take a weekend off to visit relatives. We have friends in the RAF, but she never sneaked around asking question. She didn't have time to do anything clandestine. I can't believe it's true," she added. "It's a pity that her boyfriend has also been charged."

The boyfriend referred to is Lt. Albert White (no relation of Catherine White).

Poor Bert. He wouldn't be in trouble if I'd only kept my mouth shut, Cathy thought.

She turned to the editor's column and scanned the paragraphs. "Pompous ass," she said out loud. The editorial page included spurious comments and conclusions including a quote from the Roman orator, Cicero—a nation can survive its fools, and even the ambitious. But it cannot survive treason from within.

The editor had written his column without knowing anything about her, and nothing of what she was accused of saying. Yet here he ranted about her character and her treasonable acts. Would anyone ever believe she came from the future? *Of course they wouldn't,* she told herself. *To believe that would be ridiculous.* They judged her as guilty based on the facts set out to them.

The barrister representing her intended to present evidence to refute the accusation of the crown's chief prosecutor to show that her actions, if proven to occur, did not add up to high treason. With this defense, he advised, under the *Official Secrets Act,* if the judge found her guilty of treachery, but not of high treason, she would be imprisoned for many years, but would avoid the fate of being hanged. At best, he said with a frown, they would lock her away in a mental institution to be cured of her hallucinations about being from the future.

She was tired. Tired from lack of sleep but, even more, she was weary of living these strange lives. If only she could lie down and wake up in the arms of her husband. She swore to herself that if she could return to her old life, she would hold onto him and never let him go ever again and pray she'd never again jump into the past—or the future for that matter.

There had to be a way to escape this nightmare. What had she done to deserve this? She'd progressed through so many lives, endured the arduous, grueling drudgery in those lives, and yet again, was denounced for having knowledge of future events. She should have kept her big mouth shut.

* * * *

Cathy sat, stoic, in the back seat of the plain black car. Up front were Officer Butcher and the driver. It was four in the morning when the car slowly pulled out of the cobblestone parking area at the rear of the police station, which backed on St. Andrews Street.

"Next stop—London," said the driver, a policeman in civilian clothes.

"Nice to know," Cathy snapped.

"Better take a nap," the driver said. He looked at her in the rear-view mirror. "You'll be kept busy once we get there."

Cathy didn't answer. She had no feelings left in her body. Her situation was hopeless. *I'm not going to survive this.*

The police car glided along the winding roads and passed market race tracks awaiting the dawn, when stable ved to exercise the Thoroughbred horses. They skirted the university city of Cambridge, and swept onward through the darkened countryside.

Cathy had not seen London since the blackout began. It was so strange to see the outlines of the city's tall buildings in the light of the sun now peeking above the horizon. The sight was surreal. The streets were almost deserted of vehicles— war-time fuel rationing had taken effect.

The police car drove unimpeded through the neighborhoods, some unscathed by bombings, but many were mere skeletons of flats and houses. The buildings appeared inside out with tables and chairs, still set for dinner, hanging at a crazy angle next to a wallpapered wall with lace-covered windows where the exterior walls had been peeled away. A scruffy dog loped through the bricks scattered on the side of the road, sniffing his way along the gutter. Pages from a child's book turned over in the breeze.

The sound of sirens splintered the quiet inside the vehicle. The driver pulled the car over to the curb and parked. The drone of several airplanes moaned above them.

"Crikey, sir," the white-faced driver said as he turned to Officer Butcher. "I think we're about to get bombed. We may be in danger if we stay here. What..." He turned to face ahead. At that moment, a chunk of cement crashed through the windshield, smashing the glass. Shards of glass flew into the car's interior cutting all of them, including the driver. Blood poured from his forehead and ran down his cheek. It dripped off his chin. A splinter of glass pierced Cathy's eyebrow, which immediately spurted blood. She pulled her handkerchief from her pocket and held it over the cut to staunch the flow. Officer Butcher's hands had received several small cuts. He was more angry than injured.

"We've got to get out of this car and find some cover. Quick, too," he yelled over the noise of the sirens.

Then came the ear-splitting boom, boom, boom, as bombs dropped around them. "We must move now or we'll be killed," he added. He turned back to Cathy.

"Cathy, take off your raincoat and put it over your head. It'll help a bit to protect your face and skull from falling debris out there. When I've gotten out and pulled your door open, put your head down, grab my arm, and run like hell toward that open door over here." He pointed with his head to the opening in a building that had survived a former bombing. "It's safer inside a building—no matter how destroyed. Stand in a doorway or get under some stairs."

Cathy was terrified. Bombs continued to rain down around them. Bricks and broken blocks of concrete smashed onto the top of the car bending the metal almost down onto their heads.

"We're going to get crushed," yelled the driver. "Time to get out of here!"

Butcher counted, "One, two, three," and, with a mighty shove with both his arms and feet, forced his door open. A huge chunk of masonry crashed beside him, trapping him against the car. With great difficulty, he slid along the side of the car and pulled on the rear door handle, while Cathy kicked it from the inside.

The door opened, and he immediately grabbed her arm, tugged her out of the car, and squeezed her body by the debris. Freed, Cathy covered her head with her raincoat and grabbed the officer's arm. He thrashed out with his other hand at bricks and plaster pouring down on them from the bombed building. Smoke poured out of broken windows.

Cathy saw another chunk of a terrace careening down toward her. She screamed for the men to help her. Her arms flailed around as she tried to protect her head. The action seemed like it was in slow motion. Cathy looked up as the mass came closer to her head, but was unable to ward off the piece.

Crunch. The lump crashed into Cathy's temple. Pain seared through her head.

Bang. Again, another rock smashed into her face, crushing her bones and leaving a large cut. Blood gushed from the gash.

She saw stars, and the men's faces around her turned into a blur that spun around and around as she lost blood. She collapsed onto the ground. She called out to anyone to help her. To Al, to Ed, to Alb, to Bert, to her mother, to anyone. No one came to her aid.

Help me...anyone! she screamed inside her head. Nothing came out of her mouth. *This is the same nightmare*, she thought, *only I don't think I'm going to survive this accident.*

She tried to open her eyes, but it all went into a swirling abyss—and she was sinking.

The thuds and explosions echoed in her head. It became fainter and more distant, drifting until she lost consciousness and crumpled into a heap on the ground.

The Dragonfly

PART V

The Dragonfly

Back to the present

The ambulance's siren screamed through the fog in her brain. Now where was she? In Holloway jail? The pain in her head shrieked and throbbed. Was she dead? Was she still in World War II? In the 1940s, ambulances rang bells. This was a siren. *No, I'm in a modern ambulance, so I'm almost back home.*

She was vaguely aware of movement. Her body jolted when she was transferred to a gurney and rushed into the emergency room. Bright lights flashed overhead while being moved to an empty area. It was like she was peering through a narrow passageway, with the sounds echoing through a mist. She could hear, in the distance, a doctor barking orders to several nurses milling around her body lying on a cold, stainless steel slab. Suddenly, she felt as though she were out of her body looking down on herself, floating on air.

An oxygen mask was slapped over her mouth and nose. Tubes and needles stabbed portions of her body as medical staff poked and prodded to triage her injuries. Her eyelids were pulled open and a small flashlight shone onto her pupils. Alcohol swabs stung her cuts, and glass shards were removed with tweezers. The sutures and staples stung as her large cuts were closed up.

"Wiggle your toes," called out the doctor pulling back the sheet over her feet. She complied through the haze. Then he grabbed her hand and asked her to squeeze his hand. Apparently satisfied that she had no paralysis, he ordered a CT scan of her skull. "Have to rule out head injuries," he barked.

She didn't remember how she got to the radiology department, where they pulled her off the gurney and pushed into the scanner. It was like a coffin in there—her body surrounded by the machine.

Hang on. Don't panic. I'll be out soon.

As she emerged from the scanner, the light from the huge lamp over the table pierced through her swollen eyelids. She was falling, falling into a deep well of diminishing light, until she reached a darkness where she slumbered.

* * * *

"Cathy, Cathy." A female voice penetrated the haziness in her head. Cathy moved her hand, with an IV needle taped onto the back, and touched her face. She could feel the scabs raised on the cuts on her face. *Strange,* she thought, *the cuts and gashes seemed to have healed already. The sutures and staples must have been removed.* She wrinkled her nose; she had an itch.

"Cathy, are you awake?" the female voice said.

"Yes," murmured Cathy. "Where am I?"

"You're in a hospital, dear."

Cathy forced her eyes open which seemed to have been closed forever. The nurse swabbed her eyelids with a warm liquid. They felt cleansed.

"Thanks. That helped," Cathy said, attempting to raise herself up in the bed.

"You must remain lying down, dear. You've been very ill. You must take it easy."

"I feel fine. I want to sit up."

"But…"

"Help me," Cathy demanded.

The nurse put her hands under Cathy's armpits to pull her into a sitting position and stuffed a pillow behind her back.

"Please tell me about my husband, Al White." She realized she was slurring her words because of her still-swollen lips. "Is he alive?"

"Don't worry about your husband. You have to get better yourself. You've been unconscious for quite a while, dear."

"I'm fine. I want to know about my husband. Now." *This nurse was tiresome*, she thought.

"He's fine."

"Where is he? Here at this hospital?" Cathy had been conscious for about five minutes and was annoyed already.

"I'll have to speak to Sister," the nurse answered, referring to the head nurse.

"About what?"

"So she can find out how your husband is recovering." The nurse plumped up the pillow again and straightened the bed sheet.

"Please do it as soon as you can. I've waited ages to find him, so I want to know immediately." Cathy couldn't help feeling like an irritable child about to have a tantrum. She'd gone through hell and back, and now she was so close to Al, she could almost taste it. She wanted to see him right away.

"Hello, Mrs. White." A woman breezed into her room. Dressed in navy with white piping around the collar with an air of officialdom about her, Cathy figured she must be the ward's charge nurse.

"I want to know how my husband is doing."

Sister stood at the bottom of her bed, causing Cathy to lean on an elbow in order to see her better.

"Mr. White is recovering nicely."

"Is he here? In this hospital?"

"Well, he was discharged and went home, but he comes to visit you every day. In fact, I have a surprise for you."

"What is it?"

"Nurse, please assist Mrs. White in sitting up more comfortably. She seems to have slipped down in the bed."

The nurse propped her up again, then handed her a comb and a mirror from the bedside table.

"Is he here now?" Cathy said with a broad grin.

"He'll be here in a minute or two. Make yourself pretty," the Sister said. She gave a thin-lipped smile as she swung around on her heel and left the room.

Cathy dragged the comb through her tangled hair until it ran through smoothly. She looked at herself in the mirror. *Horrors!* She had two puffy, green-and-blue bruised eyes, swollen lips, and several cuts, red but healing, on her face. She was no beauty, but she didn't care about herself. All she wanted to do was hold her husband.

There was a gentle rap on the thick, wooden door on her private room.

"Come in," the nurse called out.

An aide entered the room and held the door open. A man in a wheelchair propelled himself through the door, squeaking on the shiny, tiled floor.

"Al!" Cathy cried out. "My darling. Oh, how I've missed you."

She held out her arms to him, and he came closer, although unable to get out of the chair to touch her.

He smiled a broad smile. Relief spread across his face.

"I'm so glad to see you awake, darling." His face was bruised and his forehead bore a large, taped bandage. A hard cast was on his leg that was settled straight out on the chair's calf pad.

He wheeled over to the bed, as close as he could, and held her hand in his, cradling it like a precious gift.

"What happened? Why was I unconscious?" Cathy gazed intently at his face.

"We'll talk about the accident later, darling," Al said patting her hand. "How do you feel? You gave us a nasty scare. You received an awful bang on the head."

"I feel fine. But how are you? I thought you were dead. It was awful. I couldn't get back to you—I tried for months, but ended up back in time. Back in time. I cried so many nights." Tears ran down her cheeks while trying to tell him her story in one gushing sentence.

"Hush, darling." He tried to get his wheelchair closer to the bed. "You're a little mixed up right now. You weren't unconscious for months."

"No, I'm not mixed up. I was thrown back in history and lived through three different periods in time."

"You must've been dreaming while you were unconscious." A frown eased across his forehead.

"It wasn't a dream, Al," she whimpered. "You've got to believe me. I'll tell you the whole story when I feel better. Right now, I'm exhausted." She put her head back on to her pillows. "It's true. In each life, I met a man who looked like you. And he even had the same name."

"Why don't you try to rest now? I'll sit here until you're completely awake." He patted her hand again.

"Please stop patting me like I'm a child, Al."

He kissed her hand.

"Sorry. Didn't mean to be rude. I have a terrible headache," she said with closed eyes as she rubbed her forehead.

"I understand."

She opened her eyes and stared at him. "But...how are you? You poor darling. You look like you've been through the wars."

"I'm fine, sweetheart. Don't worry about me. You have to get yourself well."

"But your leg...looks like it's broken."

"It's on the mend. Nothing for you to fret about."

"Except I do..."

He rubbed her arm.

"Do you have a newspaper report of our accident?" Cathy mumbled through her swollen lips. "I have so many questions. Maybe that's where I should start."

"I have a copy of the Bury paper, which printed a short blurb about us," Al explained. "I don't have it here, though."

"My head aches so much. Probably won't be able to read, even if you had it."

"I'll bring the newspaper in tomorrow. I'll read it to you."

"Thanks. You're so thoughtful." She smiled as she gazed at him. Her world was normal now. She was finally back with her love, Al. *At least,* she thought, *as normal as it will ever be after her experiences during the past.*

* * * *

She quickly made progress on her path to recovery. Although she was still weak from her injuries, her head wounds had left her with no handicaps, for which everyone was thankful. The cuts on her scalp and forehead had healed and, due to the skill of the plastic surgeon, only left a faint pink scar.

Al visited her every day, and as soon as his cast was removed, walked with her in the park-like setting around the hospital. The sun shone through the trees, dappling shadows over the pathways as they moved in the warm breezes. They'd find a bench and soak in the sunshine as they chatted away the days of their recuperation.

Her doctors released Cathy after two weeks in the hospital, telling her that she now had a clean bill of health. She still hadn't told Al about her travels into the past. When she felt ready to tell him, she would. *It has to be the right time.*

* * * *

Cathy seated herself gingerly on the front seat of the new car. She was still a little reluctant to get into a moving vehicle. Any moving vehicle.

"I've found this great little pub where I'd like to take you," said Al with a smile. "We can celebrate your release…er, your discharge…from the hospital with a drink. Alone." He took her hand and kissed her fingertips.

"Somewhere new?"

"Yes. Don't know why we haven't discovered it before. It's called *The Library*. It's not far from town."

"Sounds interesting."

"I think you'll like it. It's a neat place. Cushy leather chairs, library brass lamps with green shades, and shelves packed full of old books."

"Let's go then." She pulled her hand from Al's lips and clicked her seat belt closed.

He took the back country roads to avoid traffic. They wanted to enjoy the Suffolk countryside with neat fields of wheat and a scattering of tiny villages of clustered thatched cottages. It was a lazy summer day to be enjoyed together. Al drove the car along the narrow roads at a leisurely pace. At times, the roads were so narrow it forced them to pull over to the roadside to allow an oncoming vehicle to pass.

They soon arrived at The Library, a quaint, crooked building with black wooden struts that tic-tac-toed the white-mortared walls. A new thatched roof, a foot thick, glowed golden and caressed the diamond-paned windows that appeared to be buried under the roof. The thatcher's design of cross-hatching and borders, his signature, around the roof top reminded Cathy of her mother's gold engraved bracelet. Roses billowed in full bloom around the open door.

Al helped Cathy out of the car, she resisted saying that she was no longer injured, and through the pub door. They blinked as their eyes adjusted to the dimness inside and wound their way over to a corner, where a couple of leather chairs were drawn up to a small, round table. The walls behind them held bookshelves stuffed full of ancient books.

The couple gazed around at the noisy, jovial crowd gathered at the bar. They appeared to know each other. *Probably all from the village,* Cathy thought. She shuddered.

"Are you cold, sweetheart?" Al asked as he rubbed her arm, rough with goosebumps.

"No, just remembering some of the friends I've made lately."

"What on earth do you mean?"

"The group over at the bar remind me of some of the people I met in my travels, back in time," she said quietly.

"Don't be ridiculous," he snapped. "You did no such thing. It was just a dream while you were unconscious."

The crowd became more raucous as a young woman, dressed in a white shirt, jodhpurs, and riding boots, stepped into the murkiness of the pub.

"Hullo, old girl!" called out one of the men. "How have you been? Working hard on the farm as usual? You can take the gal out of the farm, but you can't take the farm out of the gal, so the saying goes."

"Very funny," retorted the young woman as she pushed through the group toward the bar. "Some of us have to work for a living."

"That woman reminds me of my friend, Sheila."

"Hush." Al frowned.

The barkeeper moved through the crowd carrying two large plates of steaming food. "Coming through. Hot dishes here. Watch your backs." The group parted as he made his way to the table next to Al and Cathy's and set the plates down with a flourish. "This is cook's special tonight," he said to the occupants at the table. "She's the best cook around for crusted fresh trout."

"Al." Cathy, now wide-eyed, grabbed his hand and squeezed it hard.

"What?" he snapped.

"That was the cook's specialty at the manor."

"What manor?"

"In Bury."

Al frowned. "Please don't go off the deep end, Cathy."

"What on earth do you mean by 'off the deep end'?" she growled. "So you think I'm crazy? Well, thank you very much for your understanding."

"I apologize," he said quietly. "Please don't make a scene. Let's just enjoy our drink and try to relax."

She frowned at him and swung her crossed leg impatiently. He turned to look at the books lining the walls. He ran a finger along the titles. Suddenly, he stopped and tapped the spine of a book with a faded-red cover. "Good heavens!" he exclaimed. "Here's a book written by an Albert White. Same name as mine."

He pulled the hardcover book out of the row, blew the dust off the top and put it on the table. He opened the book up to the flyleaf page. "It has a copyright date of 1944," he said.

"What?" Shocked, Cathy sat up, ramrod straight, in her chair. *Can this be true?* "What's the title?"

"Strange title—*The Dragonfly—A historical time travel*."

He handed her the book, which she took gently in her hands. She opened the pages and raised the book to her nose. A familiar, almost caressing, scent drifted up to her nostrils of camphor moth balls. The memories of Bert in his blue uniform floated before her eyes.

Al took back the book. "It's about a woman's journey. She's like a dragonfly…" Al read from the introduction.

"Living through totally different stages of her life," she finished his sentence.

"How do you know that?" He looked taken aback.

She took the book from him, opened to the first page and started to read aloud.

> *As a nymph, I lived long in a watery pond*
> *Until one sunny day, I climbed a flower stem*
> *And through metamorphism*
> *I left my aquatic world and breathed in warm air.*
> *I was transformed. A second life.*

Another chance of living — a brief new life in the realm of air.
I'm a darting jewel.
Like a rainbow, my lacy wings glimmer.
Magically, my body refracts light
Into iridescent blue and green in the summer sunshine
Where faeries ride my back to shady dells.

Cathy nodded in affirmation.

"Have you read it?" asked Al.

"No, I haven't. I lived it. It's *my* story."

"What do you mean, it's *your* story?" He looked confused.

"It's a long, complicated tale, darling," she murmured as tears dropped on her cheeks. "I think I'm ready to tell you my whole story now."

Al smiled.

"I'm so happy to be here at last. I had a wonderful journey through history, with memorable people whom I'll never forget," she continued.

"Welcome home from your travels, darling."

"Thank you." She reached over, took his hand in hers, and kissed each finger. "I love you so much, Al."

She leaned back onto the high chair back as she hugged the book close to her heart, sucking in the aroma of camphor, lost in thoughts of the times past.

From the speaker in the ceiling, music floated through the pub. It was a nostalgic melody played on a flute.

Hearing the music, Al closed his eyes. "Listen, darling. They're playing our song."

BIBLIOGRAPHY

The Village Blacksmith, Henry Wadsworth Longfellow.

Jack and Jill, 17th century poem of unknown, but of suspected, English origin.

A Trial of Witches, Gilbert Geis and Ivan Bunn, (1997) Routledge, London and New York. Summary: Case study of the witchcraft trial held at Bury St. Edmunds of two women from Lowestoft, Suffolk, England. Cited as a precedent in the Salem witchcraft trials.

NOTES

Anglo Saxon Village
620 A.D.

As a little girl, the author played on the heath at West Stow in Suffolk, England. She and her cousin would find shards of pottery and arrowheads in the sandy soil.

Archeologists have since researched with several digs and discovered that the area had been occupied by stone age hunter-gatherer groups six or seven thousand years ago. The area was then used by Neolithic and Iron Age villagers. Then it contained ten pottery kilns during the Roman period, where fine pottery was produced and distributed to towns and villages far away from the village.

Two miles away is the village of Icklingham. It was occupied by Romans who built the nearby Roman road called the Icknield Way, which still remains for walkers today. See http://www.icknieldwaypath.co.uk The Romans left England around 430 AD.

The last dig revealed an Anglo-Saxon village, which was first settled in 450 AD. It's believed that many of the Romano-British population survived the collapse of Roman Britain and were absorbed into early Anglo-Saxon society, some as slaves.

The Anglo-Saxon village has been reconstructed and can be visited at West Stow, Suffolk. It's believed that the village existed until around 650 AD, at which time the villagers moved about a mile to the east around a new church.

West Stow today is centered on this new site, and the original site was gradually deserted. See:

http://www.geocities.com/Athens/2471/weststow.html

Bury St. Edmunds
1606

A stone once stood on Risbygate Street in Bury St. Edmunds. It has since been moved to the grounds of a nearby college. The common name for it is the Plague Stone, from a legend that when smallpox was raging in Bury in 1677, the socket-hole was filled with vinegar so people going home from the town market could wash their coins in it, to stop the spread of infection.

Captain Bartholomew Gosnold was the leader of the Jamestown expedition and regarded by many as the founding father of America. He was born in Suffolk and lived in Bury St. Edmunds, while his family seat was at Otley Hall, near Ipswich. This manor is beautifully preserved from Elizabethan times. See: www.otleyhall.com

Gosnold worshipped at the church, formerly known as St. James, now named the Cathedral at Bury St. Edmunds. In 1602, Gosnold led an expedition to New England and discovered and named Cape Cod and Martha's Vineyard. Martha was his daughter who was both baptized and buried at the Cathedral at Bury St. Edmunds.

See: www.stedscathedral.co.uk/exhib.htm. He named Elizabeth Island after his sister and this is where the town of Gosnold is located.

At Otley Hall, he began planning for the Jamestown colony. He was the captain of the *Godspeed*, one of the three ships in the fleet. He died at Jamestown, Virginia, on August 22, 1607, from a three-week illness. He was 36.

A skeleton was discovered at the site of the original fort at Jamestown and is believed to be that of Gosnold. It is suspected to be him because a decorative staff used by ship captains of the era and other items included in the grave.

DNA samples were taken from the skeleton and matched with the sample taken from a grave believed to be his sister's, Elizabeth. On November 19, 2005, it was announced that the DNA did not match, but it is still believed to be Gosnold buried at Jamestown because no other ceremonial objects were found in with other burials. Also, it was in a coffin that indicates someone of a higher status was buried there. http://www.historicjamestowne.org/

World War II
1939-1945

The reader may erroneously believe that a "liberated" woman is a modern term and should not have been used in the 1943 period of this novel. The expression has been in use since 1662 when a woman was described as "a witch, a charmer, and a libber." Libber had the same meaning then as today. See: Christina Larner, "Was Witch-hunting Woman Hunting?" *New Society*, October 1, 1981, p. 11

Read more about the goings-on at Shingle Street at http://www.shford.fslife.co.uk/ShingleSt/fullstory.htm

The death penalty for treason was abolished in the United Kingdom by Section 36 of the *Crime and Disorder Act, 1998*.

ABOUT THE AUTHOR

Rosemary was born in the lovely country town, Bury St. Edmunds in Suffolk County, England. You can see her home-town on her website www.Rosemary-Goodwin.com. After moving to the U.S. with her military husband, Rosemary lived in New England and currently lives in a historic town in East-ern Pennsylvania. She was a "late bloomer," attending evening classes at university and graduating law school in her late 40s.

Rosemary was first published at age twelve in her school's magazine. Since then, she's written award-winning environmental research papers on such topics as whales and uranium mining but, now that she's retired, writes mysteries, and contemporary/historical fiction.

Rosemary travels extensively in the U.S. and overseas. Of course, she returns to England every year to visit relatives and to continue researching her current projects.

To learn more about Rosemary's books, visit her website at: www.Rosemary-Goodwin.com.

For your reading pleasure, we invite you to visit our web bookstore

WHISKEY CREEK PRESS

www.whiskeycreekpress.com